Some Velvet Morning

The Final Tale Of The Blue Panda

Tree of Life Publishing

A CIP catalogue record for this book is
available from the British Library.

ISBN: 978-1-915816-13-9

Tree of Life Publishing
Devon, UK

Some Velvet Morning

The Final Tale Of The Blue Panda

Maggy Whitehouse

Other fiction by Maggy Whitehouse

The Book Of Deborah (Tree of Life Publishing)
Into the Kingdom (Tree of Life Publishing)
Leaves of the Tree (Tree of Life Publishing)
The Miracle Man (O Books)
For The Love Of Dog (Tree of Life Publishing)
Tales Of The Blue Panda (Tree of Life Publishing)
Hounds Of Heaven (Tree of Life Publishing)

Some velvet morning when I'm straight
I'm gonna open up your gate
And maybe tell you 'bout Phaedra
And how she gave me life
And how she made it end.

(Lee Hazlewood)

With thanks and acknowledgment to Dr. Margaret Barker and Ernest L. Martin for their work on researching the Hebrew First Temple.

You need to believe in things that aren't true. How else can they become?—**Terry Pratchett.**

Chapter One

SNOW CRUNCHED UNDER my boots as I walked across the churchyard. Ice crystals sparkled around my feet reflecting spangled silver in the velvet night sky above. I knew I was dreaming so this was at least semi-lucid. I also knew it was important.

My route broke new snow but there were other smaller footmarks since the last snowflakes had fallen. The scuffled snow and a few still identifiable slots looked as though a hare might have bounded into the porch of St. Raphael's and maybe taken shelter from the wind.

I shivered as a goose walked over my grave.

Above the ancient yew tree a waning crescent moon heralded the coming of dawn; I could see the outline of her full circle as well as the silver sliver. My unease intensified as I remembered another 'dream' I had had where it took so very long for the dawn to arrive. But this was such a beautiful a sight; there was a planet, maybe the morning star, Venus, just underneath the rising moon and, with the unfamiliar constellations of the pre-dawn twinkling above, it was far too breathtakingly lovely for any negative feeling or memory to sustain.

The door to the church was different; a new lighter-coloured wood replacing the centuries-old dark double-planked oak. It held a knocker in the shape of a hand pointing downwards; that ancient Islamic symbol of protection, the 'Hand of Fatima,' daughter of Mohammad. Unexpected on a Christian church. I looked up and there was a Star of David carved into the lintel above. Hmmm.

The door opened easily and yes, this was St Raphael's as I knew it—although rarely was it filled with so many pure white lilies that strangely smelled like the sweetest of roses. I've never before remembered experiencing scent in a dream but this was glorious to my appreciative dreaming nose.

9

The rood door stood open and Ariel was standing before the altar with a wreath of pink roses in her hair. The church's own angel was presenting itself as fully humanoid and, frankly, very traditional in a pale creamy shift and with light-blue raised wings. I could see every feather and I could also see an ancient, beautiful face with incredibly dark eyes. Usually I perceived Ariel as a column of light, as in C. S. Lewis's *eldils,* but this night she had hands and even feet; bare feet with toes. She laughed at my even-in-a-dream judgement that 'angels don't have feet' and I laughed, too, because she could present as anything she wanted to and if that included feet, who was I to deny it?

We exchanged energetic greetings of deep affection and she spoke.

Angels don't chat so it wasn't, 'Welcome Bel, I have something I wish to show you,' it was just Come, see but she extended a hand and I placed mine in it trustingly. Her hand felt like soft glass, cool and strong, brittle and flexible, light and clear.

See she said again, guiding me back down the aisle as if we had just been married. Standing at one side of the nave was another angel. My heart leapt as I realised this was Hero, my guardian, and she, too, was visible in human form. Hero was, surprisingly, clothed in pink but not a girly pink, more the colour of the early dawn itself. She too presented as dark haired—and as dark skinned, too, which as I'm quite dark skinned myself was, at the very least, a sign of solidarity. Very few depictions of angels are anything other than very, very white. Hero's wings unfurled as she greeted me and they were such living things! As Ariel brought her bride closer, Hero moved behind me and wrapped her wings all around my dream-body. It was lovely, soft and strong but it also made me wary that she was protecting me from something.

From your fear she said in my heart. Look.

Both angels looked up so I did, too.

St Raphael's is a Norman church nearly a thousand years old. We have the traditional effigies of the lords and ladies of the manor in the side chapels, worn-down and often indistinguishable words in the stone floor marking the resting place of other 'lesser' mortals and plaques on the walls as well. Most of them were for men and where women were honoured it was generally only as wife and mother, which frequently annoyed me. But this stone plaque was for a woman alone.

Me.

I read it carefully as Hero's wings encircled me and Ariel still held my hand.

Sacred to the memory of Rev. P. A. V. Ransom, Rector of this parish, I read. How strangely formal!

Then there was a date and beneath it one unexpected and three utterly astonishing words:

Archaeologist

Apostle of Peace.

And underneath those a sickle moon with a star, a cross and a Star of David in a row.

How in the name of all that's holy did the parish council approve *that*?

You will do this came the words into my head.

'Do what?' I asked, perplexed.

Your destiny. You will do this, was the only reply.

I woke up to the music of the alarm and, for a few moments, was lost between worlds. I swiped the 'snooze' button and lay back again, digesting that oh-so-vivid dream.

It was a lot to take in, not least because the carving in the stone had showed a particular month and a day.

It's quite something to be given the knowledge of the exact date when you will die. It wasn't a goose that walked over my grave; it was me.

'The trouble is…' said the Dean, his elbows placed sturdily on his desk and his fingers steepled, 'the trouble is…'

He paused. I couldn't blame him. I knew only too well what the trouble was and the truth, more accurately, was that the troubles *were*. They were definitely plural, hard to explain or to define and not exactly the kind of thing you could present to a diocesan council, let alone the synod.

'I expect it's ineffable,' I said, helpfully, my fingers attempting to stroke the ghost of a white German Shepherd who happened to be sitting by the side of my chair.

When I say 'white German Shepherd' I am referring to a dog, by the way, not to a Caucasian Teutonic sheep herder who might have manifested in the middle of Exbridge. Though, to be honest, that might have been easier to explain.

'Oh, I could eff it quite easily!' said the Dean, taking off the tortoiseshell half-moon spectacles that made him look like an offended owl and rubbing the bridge of his nose with the thumb and index finger of his right hand.

'Would it help if I listed the problems?' I said. 'Or at least the ones that I can articulate.'

'It's worth a try,' agreed the Dean. 'Though I'm not sure it will get us very far.'

'Okay…' I sat back in the reproduction Queen Anne chair which was intrinsically incapable of offering any comfort whatsoever no matter where you placed your backside or however you chose to lean.

'I slapped the Bishop. It doesn't matter that he slapped me first and that there's even a witness that he slapped me first; I still slapped the Bishop.'

'He's prepared to overlook that, given the circumstances.' The Dean interrupted.

'Ah yes, the circumstances.'

Simultaneously, we both reached for our blue and white Spode mugs, realised that the tea would be cold and sighed. We had been contemplating 'the trouble' for a while and passing polite conversation back and forth, which was why I knew that the Dean's mugs were Spode and that he had found them on eBay after falling in love with them while watching Judi Dench and Geoffrey Palmer in a re-run of *As Time Goes By*.

I'd discovered that the Dean preferred to be known as Xander rather than Alex as Alexander was far too long. That was Xander with an X, not a Z. Having been saddled with *Phaedra Amabel* and spending my life coping with *Faydra Annabel* I did have some sympathy. However, as the Bishop's given name is Xavier, the part of my mind that likes doing cartwheels while the sensible bit says 'shut up for God's sake,' could foresee a fair amount of confusion ahead at social situations. Luckily I'm not the sort who gets invited to those. In addition, we now had two church leaders who probably wouldn't be able to object in the least to the popular shortening of Christmas to Xmas which was going to lead to quite a lot of fun (not) with the parish council.

'More tea, vicar?' said the Dean. 'I can get a fresh pot sent in.'

'Please,' I said, ignoring the alleged joke. I could tell even on this, our first official meeting, that the Dean's sense of humour and mine were about as compatible as the Vicar of Dibley and J. D. Vance.

It was only our first 'official' meeting, by the way, because we had twice met before in the afterlife and once in a dream. Facts which we weren't even keen on admitting to each other, let alone revealing to anyone else in the diocese.

'The circumstances', incidentally, involved the Bishop's being subject to possession by a rather small but nasty demonic presence and the Dean's powers of deliverance relieving him of that embarrassing situation.

'Does he actually *know* the circumstances or is he just feeling inexplicably better?' I asked.

'The latter, I would say. It's a little bit moot and we left it hanging,' said the Dean, both helpfully and extremely unhelpfully.

'So I'm not facing any disciplinary action but it's purely because the Bishop is feeling better for no reason that he can define?'

'It's more that he has a powerful impulse not to think about the last week or so at all,' said the Dean.

'Ah.' That did make some sense. 'So that, in itself, isn't the trouble?'

'Not as such.'

'Okay. Then I guess the rest of the problem can be defined as "what do you know and what do I know and how much do we want to own up to knowing?"' I said.

'Succinctly put,' the Dean replied, before pressing the button on his intercom and asking his PA for a fresh pot of tea.

'I'll make a series of wild assumptions, then, shall I?' I said.

'If you would be so kind.'

'Okay. Wish me luck.'

'Indeed I do.'

'Right. You're an exorcist, or at least skilled at the ministry of deliverance.'

The Dean nodded.

'And so are you?' he asked.

'Not an expert but I've done a bit here and there,' I said cautiously. 'I haven't been formally trained.'

'Right. But you did know that the Bishop was possessed?'

'I suspected. I didn't know for sure.'

'And yet you got into the car with him voluntarily?'

I sighed. 'It's a long story; I was exhausted and I'd no other way of getting back home.'

'Yes… erm…' the Dean peered over his desk. 'May I ask what your right hand is doing?'

Crunch time.

'I'm stroking Margot,' I said.

'Ah!' He blinked.

There was a knock on the door and Melanie, the Dean's PA, came in to fetch the teapot, so we both overdid the thank yous and reiterated our admiration of the Spode until she had safely gone.

'Margot,' said the Dean cautiously. The ghost hound promptly left my side and returned to his.

'White German Shepherd,' I said. 'I first saw you both in Ukraine when we were clearing up after the war. She had puppies there. Before that, in an earlier incarnation, she was your dog, I believe. She's back behind the desk with you now. But then you know that.'

'Er… yes,' said the Dean. He tapped his fingers on the desk and looked at me closely. 'Well, well, well,' he said.

'We waved a few times,' I added. 'In Kiev and in Mariupol.'

'Ah.'

There was a time back in Geography class in school when the teacher was telling us how the sun was hotter when it was higher in the sky. That didn't make any sense to me and, when she asked me, in front of the class, *why* the sun felt hotter when it was higher in the sky, I answered warily 'because it's further away?'

Before everybody laughed at me, there was a particular blank look on my teacher's face. Just like the one on the Dean's right now. She had absolutely no idea how I could have reached that conclusion.

My heart sank.

As Melanie then returned with fresh tea, I have a moment to give you some background just in case you've come to this story unprepared.

My name is Phaedra Amabel Velvet Ransom. I only mention that because of the initials on the memorial plaque. Don't worry, I have forgiven my parents for the childhood trauma of having to reveal my full name in public; the constant explanations that their favourite song was Lee Hazlewood's *Some Velvet Morning* and their belief that spelling *Annabel* with an 'm' because it was French and 'different' was a good idea. I'm over the horrors of the need to write the whole thing out on every exam paper or formal application but I will admit I'm a bit ferocious if anyone spells any part of my names incorrectly. Swive it—I have to deal with it, therefore so can you! My parents died young but it wasn't my fault, honest.

To most people I'm Bel or Bella. I *am* the Rector of the parish where St Raphael's is the lead church and I *was* an archaeologist.

I'm also a soul retrieval agent in the afterlife—which is where I first met the Dean because he's one of those, too. And, momentarily at least, it was a great comfort for me to meet someone else in this same line of work because for me it all started after I had a traumatic head injury and a near-death experience and, frankly, some part of me still wonders if I'm having repeated delusions. I like these alleged delusions because I can sense and speak with angels and there is excellent job satisfaction in helping lost souls into the heavens but it's not exactly the kind of thing you can generally check out with another incarnate human being.

Every night at about 11pm, my brother Jon picks me up in his old blue Fiat Panda and drives me into the cosmos to wherever we need to go, whether it's a war zone or a private house. There we meet up with the rest of our team, Sam and Callista, and get to work on helping lost, stuck, frightened or raging souls let go of the trauma of their life and move on. I'm generally home half an hour later in Earth time with no one in my physical life any the wiser and, after a couple of years of this, I've got every reason for feeling a lot older than I look. Jon, by the way, has been dead for more than twenty years and both Sam and Callista for considerably longer.

I was engaged to be married to the old bishop. Who was murdered. I was rather involved in the trial to convict his killers which, given the trap I had set to catch them in the cathedral in Exbridge and the homeless man who rescued me when it all went tits up, got rather a lot of coverage in the news. The new bishop, consequently, found me 'challenging' and, as he managed to attract some nasty demonic energy (negative darkness doesn't like people who release souls—the deeply lost ones are food for the demonic) we ended up in an episcopal face-slapping melée in the official car. Enter Alexander Dubois, our new Dean who, as you can see, I have already met, but not in this world, who has to sort out the whole shebang and we'll take it from there, shall we? I'm sure it's quite as clear as mud.

Tea duly delivered, we looked at each other over the rims of our mugs.

'Well, back the matter in hand,' said the Dean.

There was an icy hand on my heart. He wasn't going to admit it, was he? And worse, there was a flash of horror that maybe I *was* wrong; I *was* mad (I couldn't be, I *couldn't* be; I'd learnt so much). I looked him in the eyes and tilted my head slightly, feeling mental shields forming around my body.

Hero?

Holding, she said. I knew she would be communicating with the Dean's guardian.

'I think...' said the Dean, before pausing again. Articulation seemed to be becoming a bit of a problem the other side of the desk.

'Ah,' I said, adding my share of nothing. If Xander wasn't going to engage in the subject of soul-retrieval, I wasn't going to help him with further social chat. I wasn't sure if he was denying it or if he didn't actually retain any memory of what he did in the heart of the night. I wasn't entirely sure about anything. But I didn't feel good.

'The trouble is…' repeated the Dean.

Spineless bastard I thought.

No. Good reason, said Hero.

Oh. Damn.

I sighed. 'Oh, just spit it out,' I said. 'There's obviously something you need to say—or you've been advised to say. No use beating around the bush, is there?'

'We think you should take a sabbatical,' he said, the words coming out in a rush. 'Say six months away from it all. You've been severely injured more than once recently and we're not sure if you've taken enough time to recover. And then you can consider what you would like to do next.'

'I see,' I said. 'Is there anything else or may I think this over?'

'I… I… I don't think there's anything *to* think over,' said the Dean. And to be fair, I could see that he was feeling incredibly uncomfortable.

'Take a sabbatical or there'll be "pastoral reorganisation"?'

'We wouldn't want to take it as far as that.'

Pastoral reorganisation is the church's phrase for a multitude of things including redundancy, encouraging folk to resign or moving them to a less vociferous parish.

In a nutshell, they were telling me (tactfully) that they wanted me out.

Chapter Two

'I SHOULDN'T WORRY about it right now,' said Jon that night as we flew through the solar system. He is constantly reminding me to focus on the extraordinary beauty around us as we drive to the stars in his battered old blue Fiat Panda. 'It never fails to amaze me how people would prefer to throw a load of waste words at each other instead of gazing in wonder at the glory of the Universe.'

He meant 'you' not 'people' but it was a valiant attempt at tact. And he's right; I do tend to pour my latest problems into his ears instead of realising afresh what extraordinary wonders are being set before me every time he picks me up. Humans are so weird that we can stay locked in our own problems with a supernova exploding right in front of us.

Jon and I don't *have* to drive through the night sky observing planets and stars and galaxies each time he picks me up but we do; it's a kind of way of easing me between the worlds of the living and the dead without too much of a mental-emotional implosion.

'Where to, tonight?' I said, stuffing the Dean's behaviour and my own future back down inside where they spat at me and promised to fester and to come out to bite me later.

'Towards the Horsehead Nebula,' said Jon, deliberately misunderstanding me.

'But that's more than a thousand light years away!'

'Not a problem; probably about twenty minutes,' he said. 'We've already done sixty light years-worth. And, actually, tonight isn't work; it's an office outing to celebrate.'

'You have something to celebrate?' I tried to sound enthusiastic but my foundation was feeling rocked and one of my niggly-fears for some time had been that Jon would move on further into the heavens and I would lose him again. The dead don't stay static; they move up or over or back according to the great plan for their souls. I sighed; we all have to grow and change; the nature of the universe is evolution and that includes losses as well as gains; we only get to choose whether we move willingly or have to be dragged kicking and screaming. I once heard a spiritual teacher say 'all suffering is caused by contradictions to our ego's belief of how things "should" be.' That's a tough one but I'm sure it's true. Pain is different from suffering; all lives involve pain but how we respond to it indicates how much we suffer.

The Horsehead Nebula—to Earthly probes and telescopes at least—appears to be just to the south of a star called Alnitak, in Orion's famous three-star belt. In reality Alnitak is made up from at least three stars observed in a line from Earth which is why it appears to be so bright. Of course, the three belt stars themselves are not in a horizontal row at the same distance from Earth, either. Orion and all the other constellations are a kind of optical illusion. Space, as Douglas Adams wrote, 'is big. Really big. You just won't believe how vastly, hugely, mind-bogglingly big it is. I mean, you may think it's a long way down the road to the chemist, but that's just peanuts to space.' Even more, most of the stars we see are so many thousand light years away that they may already have died. In one lifetime, we'll never know.

'We both have something to celebrate,' said Jon. 'We might even treat ourselves to a Pan-Galactic Gargleblaster.' It's not so much that he is psychic; at his level of being, like that of the angels, my convoluted human thoughts are like a visible weed-filled garden. He can spot changes of colour and mood and their meaning without having to understand the actual thoughts. We both loved *The Hitchhiker's Guide to the Galaxy* so any thought reference to Uncle Douglas sings out loud and clear.

'I could do with something to celebrate,' I said pressing my nose against the window and staring at the extraordinary vista around us.

'You mean apart from that?' said Jon pointing ahead.

It was a rogue planet, dark and mysterious and only just visible at all. They are also called 'free floating planets' or 'ISOs' meaning Interstellar Objects and, if they're large enough, JuMBOS, which is a not entirely impressive acronym for Jupiter Mass Binary

Objects. JuMBOS are strange things, lost in the nothingness of space, and no one really knows how or why they either lost their personal Sun or whether they deny ever having had one in the first place. A bit like rebellious teenagers, really. Most of them do get pulled into a loose orbit of a star eventually as they wander through space, just like most of us settle down in one way or another, but some just roam for eternity. The one we were heading for was relatively close to Alnitak Ab in Orion's Belt but, as its title implied, not tied to it in any kind of orbit.

The approach was strange. Rogue planets don't have much of an atmosphere, if any and, with no sun either, they are grey and cold. Very cold. As we flew down towards this great, dark, mass, frosting appeared on the windows and bonnet of the car.

'Is that possible?' I asked.

'Of course not!' said Jon. 'This is all multi-dimensional symbolism.'

'Ah, right.' I'd learnt some time back that further inquiry into any physical possibilities of this life-within life were incomprehensible, ridiculous and definitely ineffable but it didn't stop me asking.

We landed with a slight bump and Jon drove straight over the edge of a cliff (yes I did go 'yikes!') and down a crevasse into an even deeper darkness which seemed, like fog, to send the light from our headlights right back to us. Then there was a strange inner swirling feeling as we jumped dimensions again and now we were in what appeared to be some kind of hall where people were dancing together. They were all blurred, by which I mean I couldn't focus on them clearly; they themselves weren't so much indistinct as transparent. No one batted a non-incarnational eyelid at an old blue Panda parking on the edge of the dance floor and even I, whose previous attempts at dancing looked more like a suicidal octopus trying to pull a too-tight sweater off over its head, was willing to take Jon's hand and join in.

Once you were in the movement, and could hear the music, it was delightful; a kind of celestial cotillion-circle dance with everyone moving inwards and outwards together in harmony and a stranger taking your hand and twirling you round before moving on to whoever was next to or behind you. I knew the steps the moment we joined in though it was quite a while before I realised that my feet weren't touching any floor.

I must have held the hand of a hundred partners of all genders for just a moment before we both found ourselves dancing on. The feeling of joy was palpable; this was a dance of love and delight. I would have been happy to have existed in this melody forever.

Occasionally I became aware of Jon still being close beside me and I saw him becoming younger; his clothing transformed into (a comfortable version) of a Regency gentleman's magnificence. I, too, was changing in appearance; from jeans and sweatshirt into some wonderful silky Arabian-style pantaloons, a silky blouse with floating sleeves and some kind of waistcoat. I could have sworn I was wearing some sort of turban, too. It wasn't only the clothes; I could feel myself stretching as though growing taller and my body was flowing and flexible as water.

All at once the music changed, becoming more processional, and I found myself dancing in a four with Jon and two others whom I (just) managed to recognise as being our partners-in-*not*-crime, Sam and Callista. Usually they looked as human as I but tonight they were flames of transparent fire disguised as Victorians. I know I was looking directly at two immortal souls and for a moment I found myself wishing my soul were that bright.

'Of course it is, you prune,' said Jon, himself afire beside me. 'If it weren't you couldn't even perceive us like this.'

Then all thought was forgotten as we turned and twirled in this incredible dance, our hands and spirit bodies flowing into each other. I'd say it was breath-taking but I have no recollection of actually breathing in this higher world.

In one smooth movement Jon, Sam and Callista flipped me so that I flew for a moment above the dance hall, immersed in light and warmth before coming to rest before a being of indescribable beauty. I have no idea if she were human, angel or some other being—or even if she were a 'she'—but s/he presented in tall, glowing golds and pinks that flowed around her in a way that expressed both love and strength.

'**Yes**,' she said as eyes as dark as night, yet light as day looked into and through me. '**Yes, it is time.**'

From then on, it becomes hazy in my mind. I was aware of being the equivalent of a child in a very magical but grown-up Universe. I was aware of Jon, Callista and Sam being honoured in some way and thanked and invited to... to something, perhaps another level? Whatever it was, their eyes were shining and they were so filled with joy—as was the air around us with the other dancers offering cheers like the sound of cascading waters and the most beautiful bird song.

Hearts can't sink in this place; egos are gone and my heart knew it was all right and true and perfect and I also knew *somehow* that it was not yet. Like being given a university place and knowing it was being held for you until you were ready to say 'yes.'

I somehow also knew that none of them would be moving on until I did.

And then it was my turn. Now we seemed to be in another hall; smaller and with fewer people but the angelic human was there and focused on me. I know s/he offered me three scenarios. I had work to do, a destiny to fulfil, but I had choices. I remember thinking that I had no idea you could have a choice of your destiny and knowing in reply that all strands would be completed eventually but, even so, choice was needed now. I was able to perceive three life paths that I could follow on Earth and three deaths. I could see the help I would receive and the obstacles in my path. With the angel beside me and Jon, Sam and Callista beside me, I chose.

I have absolutely no idea what path I selected.

Usually, after a night's work, Jon drives me back to my Earthly home but this time I simply woke up the following morning, refreshed and filled with a sense of purpose. All of which crashed and burned when I remembered the meeting with the bloody 'Avoid-the-critical-subject-Xander-with-an-X' Dean and how I had to get my mind around what to do and where to go for six months. Realistically, I wasn't going to be able to stay here because that would get in the way of my assistant, Lucie, or whoever they might send to fill my boots. And, worse, people would still be 'just dropping in' to tell me how much better/worse Lucie was doing and to offload their thoughts to me because that was their normal practice. Not to mention the issue of a parishioner falling ill and wanting to see me. Or what I'd do about phone calls from people who knew this as 'the vicarage'? And what to do about emails? I've got a work account and a private one but I haven't been as wise about boundaries there as I should have been.

'Oh damn it, it'll work out; have some bloody faith,' I told myself as I stepped into the shower. 'You've got some kind of a 'destiny' to fulfil and you know it, which is more than ninety per cent of the population does… and doing whatever that is, is probably going to take you a while. You can get started in the next six months—once you find out what it actually is!—and *then* you can decide what to do next.'

I did some serious thanksgiving while I washed my hair. I have an extraordinary life; I can see angels; I have beloved friends; I have experienced love on Earth and in Heaven and I've survived more bangs on the head than you could shake a stick at. Though please don't shake a stick at me because given my luck, you'll miss and give me another one.

My thanksgiving, however, is always slightly limited as there is still a significant area of my life which is lost. That's thanks to one of the aforementioned head injuries; the one where I died and came back. The love of my life (according to everyone else, that is, because I can't remember if he actually was) is in those lost memories. I can only recall the last time he and I met on Earth when I'd completely mislaid the fact that we were lovers and were planning to get married. He was incredibly kind to me then, realising that I had no recall and still loving me and allowing me to meet him again for the very first time. I fancied the socks off him and, occasionally, in the heart of the night when I'm alone I can half-imagine half-recall what it might have been like to make love with him. And yes I do act it out, because I'm only human.

My actual husband is a complete mystery to me. I've no idea why I was attracted to him; what our marriage was like (eight years, apparently) or why we broke up. Occasionally people expect me to dislike or be angry with him but I can't. He's just some bloke who lives within my parish, is happily married to his second wife and has two kids whom I've Christened. The latter is a little surprising as Galel is a Muslim but maybe he believes, as I do, that God is a tad bigger than human ideas of religion.

Once cleaned up and breakfasted, I did what I always do—and am privileged to be able to do—I set off to see the local witch.

Chapter Three

ALESSINA BENNETT IS definitely a witch. She is also my best friend which is something I'm rather proud of, to be honest. Of course there's the utterly childish 'neener-neener' aspect to it as in 'Look at me, the vicar, being friends with a witch' whenever I'm with the Parish Council—I'll totally admit that the said PC does bring out the worst in me because they're not PC in any other way. Alessina, fortunately, doesn't know that aspect. Most of her witchy friends are fairly dismissive—and angry—with Christianity, with good reason. After all, it's my 'tribe' that burnt their 'tribe' at the stake and if I, in some past life, had any part in that, I am truly sorry. Luckily, Alessina and I manage not to play tribe; we have arguments and heated discussions for sure but at the heart of it we believe in one creation and one creator and in the power of love. We simply call it by different names. In fact, I would say that Alessina's Way has far more love for our Mother the Earth than Christianity has ever shown. Yes, St. Francis is the exception but our record hasn't been great, has it?

Alessina also keeps me believing that I am (relatively) sane. She has met and spoken with Jon; she can see and communicate with angels and demons and she even saved me with a fabulous exorcism where she spat holy water-infused elderflower champagne over the possessed man who was threatening me. That man was my former assistant vicar, Robbie, who is all that is good and hopeless and inarticulate and devoted in a minister but who, like most of us, had a vulnerable spot which was exploited when he wasn't looking. Robbie now has his own parish in the Fens where he rides his bicycle everywhere, even though he often forgets his specs and can barely see road signs. The lurcher he recently adopted from the Dogs Trust trots alongside and charms all his parishioners with smiles and hairy kisses. Caractacus (what a name!) adores

Robbie and slowly both are beginning to realise that they do not only have to give love; it is more than reasonable to receive it too. Robbie's self-doubt isn't helped by the fact that he is, basically a stick insect with a bad comb-over. He probably *would* get eaten by any mate but I do pray that one day he will be found by One with a heart as good as his and eyesight just as bad. Maybe he could come and be my locum for six months? I wouldn't have a problem with Robbie staying in my house. I should, here, explain that unlike most vicars I have my own home. Lucie lives in the parish house down the road. My house *is* the old Rectory so it's logical that people think it belongs to the church.

Alessina was busy. Of course she was! She has clients nearly every day seeking to rediscover their souls in a world where Christianity has focused on sin and duty. I often go down to her witch's cottage anyway, whether or not she is going to be free, and hang out with the spirits in the garden even if I can't get to see my friend. Sometimes her husband Luke is there; sometimes her adult children. They kindly let me mooch around the garden or make myself a cup of tea (quietly) in the kitchen if she isn't going to be long. Otherwise I talk to the fairies a little, which seems only polite even though they are invisible to me, and then walk back home. It is a truly glorious walk along a footpath overhung by oak, goat willow and hazel with the moor visible on one side and deeper woods and a gabbling stream on the other.

This time, I didn't wait but headed back and walked straight into Simon the Woodsman. It was a shock. We had met before but not in this dimension; I'd slipped into some kind of parallel universe for a while and he had given me a vital clue—and a warning—as to work I had to do there. Maybe he was a spirit man who could walk between worlds because it was definitely the same man and I was pretty sure I was still in my own time and place. Yes, I know it's weird in my world. I was going to add 'but it's the only one I've got' but that would be palpably untrue.

Simon was wearing exactly the same clothes as I remembered, a jacket and trousers that once had been black but had weathered into that soft dark grey which is such a fine camouflage for the woods.

I went 'Oh!' as we almost collided. He said nothing; I wasn't sure he even recognised me but for some reason I knew I needed to speak with him.

'Simon?' I said. 'It's Bel, "the Lady of the Yew."' That's what he had called me the other time we had met.

He stopped and looked me up and down with those clear Celtic blue eyes. He didn't know me. I felt a right prat.

'Excuse me,' he said kindly, intending to walk past.

'I found the souls,' I said. I knew I was gabbling but I couldn't stop myself. I even put out a hand to touch him on the arm.

'You gave me four yew arils and warned me of danger. You were right but it was okay in the end. I got them through. Me and my dog.' The 'dog' was Seraphim, actually a hound and my beautiful ghost dog for several months. Yes, I *know* 'Seraphim' is a plural but that was her name and if you're going to have a funny name yourself you kind of have to accept others with similar.

He stopped and turned.

'I do not know you,' he said. 'But I'll accept you know me from another time and place. I have no message for you now—wait!' He stopped speaking and seemed to listen.

'He'll come after the moon is full,' he said. 'That's all I know but it is more than enough.'

'Who will come?'

'Your Anam Cara. Good day to you, Miss.' He walked on while I stood entranced. My Anam Cara! My soul friend or soul mate, as in John O'Donohue's wonderful writing. Suddenly the day was brighter—I wandered on the edge of the moor enjoying the autumn sunshine and the dappling of the light through the trees. Meandering is one of my contemplative practices; I don't think we should 'hike' in the countryside; we should wander and watch and wait and glory in all that is beautiful. I sat for a while watching a wren while feeling the joy that Simon's news had given and, probably for the first time in quite a while, felt truly relaxed. That is, until I remembered I had a funeral visit and a Parish Council meeting still to come so I'd better get back home and try to look respectable.

Funeral meetings are never easy and, surprisingly, the ones

where there isn't much grief can be even harder than the ones where the loss is deeply felt. This was one such. Maisie Fenwright had been quite a fearsome beast, one of those tough women you often find running a riding stables where little girls work on a Saturday morning in a meld of delight and terror that they'll get something wrong. Her word was law. She would shout at anyone who got in her way, was—frankly—mean to her only daughter as well as being one of those lunatics who keep going no matter what and expect everyone else to sacrifice themselves, too. My weird patchy memory could recall the time she broke a leg and cut the plaster off herself after two weeks because she 'couldn't be doing with it' any more. Her leg still set; it wouldn't have dared not to.

Maisie spent fifty years hunting, drag hunting, cross-country racing, terrifying the children who came to Pony Club and hacking across the moors berating anyone who got in her way. She finally gave up riding at the age of eighty-seven when her beloved horse, Folly, died and Maisie dropped dead herself six months later.

'How are you doing today,' is my usual doorstep question for the bereaved. I put a slight emphasis on the 'today' as some days are better than others; some are almost bearable and some are the most terrible you can imagine.

'Relief,' said Maisie's daughter, Connie. 'Pure, joyful relief.'

'Oh?'

'God yes. I'm finally free. I can sell the bloody stables, find decent homes for the older horses, move out of this dump and get a life.' Fair enough, I suppose. Connie had been Maisie's virtual slave for years. God knows why she never moved away, got a job or found a partner but she never had. She appeared to have accepted a sixty-year version of slavery.

'Come on in, Reverend. My cousins are in the living room. They'll say all the right things and I'll behave but I can't tell you a lie. I'm glad the bitch is gone.'

O…kay…

They all did say the right things and the youngest of the cousins did shed a tear (how odd to be saying that seeing a tear was actually a relief in a funeral planning meeting) but apart from Maisie's love of horses and her brief marriage to Clive, who had gone off with the next door neighbour six months after Connie was born, no one really had a thing to say.

'I don't know why we don't have one of those *Just Cremations*,' said Cousin Fenella. 'It would be so much easier *and* cheaper.'

'Mother wanted to be buried in the churchyard,' said Connie patiently. 'It's in her will. You can't go against her will.'

'I don't see why. She's dead. She won't care,' said Fenella.

She might, I thought but, obviously, kept quiet.

'Well, actually this *is* cheaper,' said Connie. 'Mum's body is in the mortuary at the hospital because there had to be a post mortem and they'll keep it there until the funeral. We don't need a funeral director. I'll get a cardboard coffin off eBay and pick her up in the van on the day, take her to the church. We can carry the coffin in ourselves and then she's buried. There's only the vicar's and the burial fee and we already have the plot because we bought a family one when Grandpa died.'

I sat quietly marvelling. Funeral directors' fees are huge nowadays and even *Just Cremation* costs about £900. This sounded perfectly feasible; I guess it ends up being about whether the mortuary folk are kind and whether you're happy to organise the coffin and carry it. Connie was as tough as her mother by the sound of it.

The money discussion continued while I drank my tea and tried not to eat the biscuits. They weren't very interesting biscuits and I would get far better at the Parish Council meeting but it's so horribly tempting to nibble to pass the time when relatives are arguing across you.

Fortunately, Connie put her foot down by asking if they wanted the vicar to charge overtime while they wasted time (vicars don't charge overtime but we probably should). Again, I kept quiet.

And then the bombshell.

'There's something you all should know,' said Connie. 'I only found out myself from reading the will. Mum married again.'

'*What? Who?*'

'Someone called Benjamin Fairfax. I don't know how or when

but he's mentioned in the will — thank God she didn't leave him everything! She remade her will after the date of the wedding and he's not even mentioned. But there's a wedding certificate. It's a really weird one and I have no idea if it's even valid but I suppose he might turn up to the funeral.'

'Well they certainly didn't live together! When was this? Who is this man?'

'I have no idea. The certificate says he's an archaeologist so he could be anywhere.'

Another cup of tea was mooted and appropriate levels of outrage were expressed. I thought it was rather amusing but I politely kept my mouth shut. That is until Connie showed me the marriage certificate which hailed from the State of Utah.

'It's an online marriage,' she said. 'I looked them up. You can get married anywhere in the world online nowadays. What do you think of that?'

'Is that actually legal?' I asked. 'There's all sorts of stuff you have to do and all sorts of information you have to provide before you can get married.'

'Who knows?' said Connie. 'All I care about is that he doesn't think he'll be getting anything and he doesn't contest the will.'

The certificate was dated five years earlier so this man had obviously been in Maisie's life for quite some time.

'And do you even know who he is?'

'Not a clue. And as I said, I don't care.'

'Did he get anything at all in the will?'

'Not a sausage.'

That was odd, too. But no one had any more to say about it apart from deriding Maisie further. We progressed to the job in hand and I fell back on the old standard questions that I keep in mind for the saddest funerals where the person's life appeared to be completely unlived apart from that one-size-fits-all phrase 'loving wife/husband.' No one here had stories they wanted to tell. Maisie's life *had* been lived but among herds of horses so from the human point of view this was almost as blank.

'Where was she born?'

'Here.'

'How did she do at school?'

'Don't know.'

'What were her other hobbies?'

'Nothing. Just horses.'

'Did she travel?'

'No.'

'Not even to Utah?'

'No, it was done online. I showed you.'

'Do you have any funny stories about her—about either of her weddings perhaps?'

'No.'

'Any childhood memories you'd like to share?'

Silence. 'No, not really.'

'Did Maisie have any faith?'

'No. She just wanted to be buried in the churchyard with her parents.'

'Aha—can you tell me about her parents?'

No one here had ever met Maisie's parents. They bustled around to find an old photograph album to show me but it wasn't going to help with the eulogy.

'And you have no contact with your Dad at all?' I said, carefully to Connie.

'No idea if he's alive or dead,' she said, cheerfully.

'O-kay… So would any of you like to speak at the funeral?'

'God no!'

That bit was fair enough. We vicars are used to public speaking but most people would run a mile. Jerry Seinfeld had a joke about how the top two fears in America were public speaking and death which meant that when it comes to a funeral, most folk would rather be in the coffin rather than doing the eulogy.

It was a slight relief to move on to the service itself. Just the normal church service, thank you. No, no flowers. No one else to speak. No poems; no pictures. I did my best, I always do, but I knew I would have to write a eulogy out of nothing unless I could find a soul who had actually *liked* the woman. I was pretty certain there would be people who'd loved riding who would have a good word to say; maybe I could go down to the hunt and ask there—but it was going to be a lot of extra work. I'd do it because that's my job but I don't like having to research someone's life outside the family.

'Is there any other family I could speak to, at all?'

'You mean apart from this Benjamin? said Cousin Jessica. 'No. And we don't know where he is. He's apparently on some archaeological dig somewhere in the Middle East.'

'So does he know she's dead?' I *really* should have asked that one earlier.

'I sent him a text,' said Connie. 'His number was in Mum's phone. He didn't reply.'

'Do you think he might he have any stories about your Mum?'

'I shouldn't think so. I've never even met him. Don't think he's ever even been here.'

Curiouser and curiouser.

'Right... So... do you mind if I ask for any stories that village people and Maisie's riding pupils might remember?'

'No.'

'Okay, well I'll work on a eulogy—probably quite a short one—and let you see it towards the end of the week then. And maybe I should call this Benjamin?'

'Oh no, don't worry about that. I'm sure whatever you write will be fine. We don't need to read it,' said Connie. The cousins agreed.

I left feeling flattened. How could a whole life end in such indifference, if not hostility? And why was there no contact or even interest in the alleged husband? (I was aghast at the idea of online weddings and knew I'd be researching them half the night). Stopping at the post office for a comforting bar of chocolate I asked Patsy the postmistress if she had any memories of Maisie Fenwright.

'Rude. Pushy,' she said. 'Not my favourite customer.'

'Right...'

I know, I thought. I'll ask the Parish Councillors. I bet they can find something. And with that I went home to put the kettle on for a cuppa before walking down to the parish house where Lucie lives and the PC was about to meet for 'an issue of concern to the whole parish' (oh joy!) and most likely to berate me for something weird that I'd done, again. My phone pinged a text just as I got there. *Stuck in triffid. Be there in net minuets.*

I should mention that Lucie is dyslexic and relies on autocorrect *far* too much.

The Parish Council is made up from Balding Tortoise Man (Colin), Angst Ridden Fidgeter (Diana), Aristocratic Nose Man (David), Jolly Ruddy-Faced Man (Joe) and Awkward Redhead (Sara-pronounced-Sarah). That's not why she's awkward, Sarah is vegan, about which none of us has the slightest problem but she *never* stops going on about it. Sara objects to the church's beeswax candles *and* soy candles because beeswax abuses bees and soy is genetically modified and used to feed cattle cruelly incarcerated in sheds. Normal candles are detested, too, because they come from the petrochemical industry. She's right on all fronts but I'm not having fake candles in the churches—plastic is just as bad, right?—so beeswax it is even if harvesting honey and wax is harmful to bees. My own argument that given the state of bees due to pollution and pesticides, bee-keepers who maintain good hives and harvest honey and wax is a good idea in order to keep the population going, simply doesn't wash.

Together the PC makes a formidable brick wall against any progress in the Church-with-a-big-C, the church itself or the parish. *Always* they disagree… and those very disagreements have created impasse after impasse, whether it was about the suitability of having 'heathen' yoga classes in the church hall or—heaven forbid!—removing the pews in any church whatsoever. I particularly have to watch my ingestion of biscuits at Parish Council meetings as keeping my mouth full of sugar is practically the only way of stopping myself gnawing my fingers off with frustration.

Individually each councillor is a stalwart of the parish and a perfectly nice person, as long as you take the original meaning of 'nice' as derived from the Latin *nescius*, meaning 'unaware or ignorant.' It isn't that they are actually horrid but they are isolated, life-long Devonians who have never had to cope with more than the very occasional person of colour or another religion and they are institutionally and completely unconsciously racist. The Church of England and the Methodists tolerate each other down here though Catholics are rare and seen as oddities. There are synagogues in Exbridge and Plymouth but they are almost as empty as the churches and Galel, my ex, is the only Muslim we know of in the parish. And I, as a mixed race vicar, am — even after years in the job —considered alternatively a cute anomaly and a dangerous radical.

Lucie they adore but then *everyone* adores Lucie, including me. She drives me nuts as well but that's because I'm a raddled old cynic and she is gentle positivity with wings. Lucie could take part in an 'adopt an abandoned vicar' advertisement and her radiant beauty and goodness would have people turning up on our doorsteps to carry us off and love us to death. I'm not sure why the ailing Church of England hasn't realised that and chosen her as its mascot.

Then again there could be the issue of tact, I suppose. Lucie did take me to task over my self-appellation of 'mixed race.' Apparently I should be saying *someone with a mixed ethnic background* or 'someone from the mixed ethnic group' or, maybe, 'a person of colour.' When I said I didn't give a shrive about the latest PC terms, I *was* brown and I didn't need a pink person to tell me what I was, she actually cried for me. *She* cried for *me!* (and told me so).

This is the woman who, when she turned off autocorrect after she realised she was sending confusing texts, promptly texted me that she had driven past KFC and bought a massive amount of nuggets and did I want to come round to share them and watch a DVD? To be fair, U is next to I and R is next to T and I was far more offended by the idea that I'd eat chicken nuggets than any unintended racial slur. She has since turned autocorrect back on.

I have a key to the church house although it feels awkward to use it when Lucie is out as it is also her home. However, the Cause Of The Meeting was already standing outside the house with pursed lips and a briefcase which was probably full of documents. Let's call him 'Mr Complaint' because that's what he was intending to do.

I let him in and sat him down and refused to let him start

talking by telling him it would be unfair for the others not to hear all he had to say and then hid in the kitchen until the others turned up.

We convened courteously. It's fair to say that half of the PC is at war with the other half as well as with the 'modern world.' Occasionally I ask them questions like, 'If you can't negotiate a peaceful settlement between Christians from the same parish, how to you expect warring countries and religions to do so?' or quote Jesus' seventh Beatitude: 'happy are the peacemakers.' I can be quite fierce at times so they do always *convene* courteously. Although it is important to have the right biscuits to start with; Rich Tea for tradition's sake, Jammie Dodgers or Bourbons (both vegan) for Sara, chocolate hobnobs because chocolate is essential and one other 'surprise' biscuit so they can enthuse or dismiss it according to their wont.

At the end of the meeting, given that Colin is the chairman and prone to waffling and wandering off on red herrings, it's usually me who has to call them back into focus and ask for a vote. But he's a good starter, that's for sure, and makes sure that 'the girls' (which usually means Joe and Lucie as, understandably, the other 'girls' tend to bristle) get us sorted with tea and individual plates and paper napkins for our biscuits and gets the minutes passed with style.

Today, we were introduced to Mr Complaint as being Norris Whipple from St. Michael's towards the far end of this band of parishes. Mr Whipple accepted a cup of coffee, declined a biscuit and launched. There was a deeply concerning increase in alternative therapies and practitioners of healing and magic throughout the area, he said. And it had come to his attention (don't you just love that phrase) that the Rector, *the Rector!*' he said, looking daggers at me, 'is actually *consorting with a witch!*'

Oh God, here we go…

Chapter Four

DON'T GET ME wrong, there are plenty of alternative practitioners out there who are mad, bad and dangerous to know. There are also more than a few doctors who are just as crazy, if only in the arrogance stakes where they assume that scientific evidence is the only answer to everything—if there is a known answer, that is. When there isn't one, then the dis-ease is deemed incurable or chronic and all that 'can be done' is pain relief. Plenty of dis-ease is caused by aspects within us that doctors are never taught about and, if they were, they would probably dismiss. I was once told that medical training included one day on nutrition. I have no idea if that is still true but my own experience of hospital food shows that, in so many cases, the finances are more important than nourishing food—or anything else.

We humans love to assume that everything our five senses and our rational brains can detect is all that there is. We can perceive all of the 'visible light spectrum' but the key word there is 'visible.' Most of it is invisible, to us at least. There's plenty that science knows about but can't identify, including dark matter. Humans can't take in the vast scale of the universe, nor can we perceive the atomic structure of matter. There is plenty of radiation we can't see, at wavelengths shorter and longer than visible light.

But I digress. We were talking about alternative—or complementary—medicine practitioners. There are also plenty of good-natured souls with perfectly valid training and techniques which may very well help a lot of people, particularly those that the orthodox medical system leaves behind. And there are plenty of folk, too, who think that vicars or imams or rabbis are deluded and harmful (and some of us are).

Basically, if you watch the TV you'll find that there is an ongoing witch hunt against complementary medicine and all the ancient techniques in our dramas. That's exactly what it is; a witch hunt. The practitioner is nearly always shown to be corrupt, deluded or harmful. Folk who call themselves witches particularly are pilloried and, yes, there are stupid people who hang charms and dream-catchers everywhere and dabble in esoterica and even Satanism without the slightest idea what they're messing with. But TV perpetuates the bad name of the witch and in all the wrong ways. She (and it usually is a she) is either a weirdo laughing-stock or a dangerous fake-magical figure. A wise woman who does only good in the world is not the most common perception. I have wrestled words with Alessina about this, suggesting she calls herself a shamanic healer rather than saying outright that she is a witch but her argument was valid.

'How do we redeem the word "witch" without living what it truly means?' she said. That in itself is a conundrum as there are so many possible sources of the word, from *wiccan, wiccian* or *wicce* (magician or sorcerer), *wiggle* (divination). There's also the Proto-Germanic *wikkiaz* (necromancer). Alessina's interpretation is rooted in the Gothic German terms *weihs* which means 'holy' and *wehan* which means 'consecrate.' She's right, too, in that the priests and priestesses of any superseded religion are virtually always damned as magicians by their successors. The word 'pagan' simply means 'country dweller' but to Christianity it means heretic. And that's one of the reasons we lost our all-important connection to the land which has led slowly and inexorably to our lack of care for our planet's essential welfare.

Did I say all this to the Parish Council? No, because it would be banging my head on a brick wall and my head has been damaged enough already. What I did do was go to the heart of the matter.

Outside the window, a glorious scarlet storm-cloud sunset was boiling over the hills. Pathetic fallacy?

'To whom are you referring? I said with beautiful and somewhat arsy grammar.

'That Mrs Bennett down the Dell,' he answered. 'That friend o'yorn as you well know.'

'I see. And what do you *mean* by accusing her of being a witch? To what are you actually referring?'

'Well, it's magic, b'ain't it? Spells and 'erbs and stuff. And it's un-Christian!' he said, warming to the subject.

'What magic?' I asked.

'Well I don't know, do I? But everyone knows she does it.'

'Mr Whipple, what everyone knows is not evidence,' said Colin (bless him).

'Well, *spells!*'

'What kind of spells?' I asked.

'She put a curse on my chickens!' Norris was practically foaming at the mouth by now.

Colin was about to speak but I put my hand up.

'Why would she do that?' I asked.

'Because she'm a *witch!*'

'Even witches—and I'm not saying Mrs Bennett *is* a witch— would need a reason. Have you done anything that might have upset her.'

'O'course not!'

'Well then she'd have no reason to curse your chickens, would she?'

'She'm a witch,' he said.

'Norris, your chickens got bird flu,' said Colin. 'It was unfortunate but Mrs Bennett had nothing to do with it. Not that I approve of her,' he added.

'Does she need our approval?' I said.

'You'm the vicar!' said Norris Whipple. 'It ain't Christian.'

'People go to Mrs Bennett for healing when their doctors can't help them,' I said, as gently as I could. 'Christ healed those who could not be helped by official methods. He was a heretic to his own people. I don't see any harm in anyone else being a healer.'

'She b'aint a Christian!'

'Sadly, very few people are nowadays,' I said. 'And might I refer you to chapter nine, verse forty nine in the Gospel of Luke?'

'Eh?'

'"John answered and said, 'Master, we saw one casting out devils in your name; and we forbade him, because he does not follow us'. And Jesus said unto him, 'Forbid him not: for he that is not against us is for us,'"' I quoted. 'Mrs Bennett is definitely not against us. Although, if she *is* a witch, as you claim, she would have good reason to be against us. We Christians burnt witches at the stake, if you remember.

'Incidentally, are *you* a practising Christian, Norris? I don't think I've ever seen you in church.'

'Of course I am!' Norris was deeply offended.

'I wouldn't mind if you weren't,' I said. 'That's the difference between us. Jesus was very clear that we were meant to follow him—to heal, to love and to reconcile. Even though the Church of England teaches that we should worship him, he never once asked us to do so. He asked us to *follow* him. Now, do you have any evidence whatsoever that that is exactly what Mrs Bennett—in her own slightly unorthodox way—is *not* doing?'

'She'm a witch,' he said again.

'Mr Whipple, do you have any evidence?' said Sara. 'If it's all hearsay… I'm not saying I approve of Mrs Bennett but…'

'My chickens,' said Norris again. 'She cursed 'em! And… and… well I'll find some, don't you worry! And what about they Yoga folk and they acupuncture people in our church halls? You can't tell me that's right!'

'Why not?' I said, dangerously. 'What exactly is wrong with them?'

'It's heathen magic!' said Norris like a toy train running round and round the same track. There's nothing you can do to change someone's mind when they're stuck in the groove of self-righteousness. Facts simply don't work.

'Well, I agree that it's rubbish,' said Diana with one of those annoying little laughs. 'At best it's the placebo effect.'

'To which complementary medicine discipline are you referring?' I said. My back was definitely up. Hero was whispering in my mind, telling me to step back, to relax, but I wasn't listening.

'Well, all of them!' she said with wide eyes. 'They're all hokum and often harmful.'

'Acupuncture?' said Joe, warily. 'I hear that can be quite helpful.' I knew for a fact that his wife's chronic migraines had been sorted through acupuncture and, I gathered from Lucie, who was currently listening with her head on one side and an elegant eyebrow raised, that the treatment had also restored the couple's sex life. A fairly dramatic win for acupuncture, I would have said.

'Pshaw!' said David. 'My wife had someone at the sports club put hot stones on her back. Said they were healing! Surrounded her with bits of rock as well calling them *shaky*-or-something crystals. Utter rubbish.'

'Chakra,' I said icily. 'An ancient Eastern tradition of balancing within the body's nerve ganglia.' Well that was a wrong move, wasn't it?

'Are you one of them Muslims?' asked Norris accusingly. To the Rector of his parish. Sometimes I despair.

'No, I'm a vicar,' I said. 'You might have noticed if you came to church sometimes.'

'Now, now,' Colin held up his hands in a movement both commanding and placatory. 'Enough of all this. Norris, what is the *specific* issue you want to address? Generalities are of no use.'

'*We*,' said Norris, upping the stakes considerably. '*We* want this alternative stuff banned from church halls at the very least. And *we* want that Mrs Bennett removed from the parish.'

'Who is "we" please?' said Lucie.

'Oh you'll find out!' said Norris and, for the first time, I saw another energy behind him. Shit. This wasn't just an outraged nincompoop, this was serious.

'We cannot simply request someone to move out of the area!' said Sara. 'I'm sure we can do something about the practitioners using our church halls. We can, at least, take a vote to ban them.'

'A blanket ban,' said Norris in a loud and assertive voice. 'That's a start.'

'Mr Whipple,' I said. 'You are not a member of this parish council. Your views have been heard. We will debate them. Now, if you would be so kind, we need to conclude our business.'

I stood up and moved towards the door to open it.

Norris Whipple jumped out of his chair and grabbed my wrist.

'You'm a witch too,' he hissed. 'We'll get you, too. You'll see. You'm next on our list.'

'What list?' said Lucie, getting up and firmly removing his

hand from my arm. 'And who are "we"? Mr Whipple, I advise you strongly to calm down, sit down and clarify. What list and who are "we"?'

'Ha!' said Norris and stomped out of the room slamming the door behind him.

'Thank you,' I said to Lucie. I felt quite shaken.

'Well!' said Diana and Joe together. '*Well!*'

We had another cup of tea while the PC debated whether or not a ban on alternative therapies on Church premises was a good idea. I stayed silent and prayed. This was a threat; a palpable threat to Alessina and possibly to me. And I was due to take a sabbatical which meant I wouldn't even be able to stand up for her with the weight of the Church at my back. Even worse, my leaving now could be seen as a sign that I wasn't to be trusted. I had considered telling the PC that I would be going away but I needed to talk with Lucie first. Now I simply didn't know what was best.

Prayers work but (a) in their own time, not ours, and (b) sometimes the answer is 'no.' In this case, it was a 'what do I *do?*' and the answer was hidden in my anxiety. I'd understand when I was calmer and on my own without all this confusing energy flying around the room.

As I sat, I watched Lucie. She was steadily growing into her own skin and belief in a way that shone; not that Lucie even needed more shine. I tried to remember her age—was it twenty-seven or twenty-eight? Whichever, she now had poise and increasing confidence. When she arrived in the parish she was afraid to say boo to a goose but now she was handling the PC with kindness and clarity. I caught her eye and she flashed me a smile. Both she and I knew that I was best out of this debate because I *was* friends with a witch.

No final conclusion was reached but 'advice was to be taken' from folk around the parish as to their views. The trouble with democracy is that issues often get kick-started by one person who then rounds up people who'd never really thought about it and didn't know they were supposed to object but who are happy to be offended on cue. Fair enough, most of us don't think about things much but being rounded up and pointed in the direction the leader wants to go isn't helpful either. And Norris Whipple obviously had every intention of rounding people up, if he hadn't already.

Lucie walked back to the Old Rectory with me. 'I know why Mr Whipple thinks Alessina cursed his chickens,' she said. 'He blocked off the footpath by her house. It's a public footpath but he put up an electric fence when some people left a gate open.'

'Oh, yes I remember. She told me about it. She complained to the council and they made him put a stile over it with those protective covers but they didn't make him take the electric fence down.' I didn't add Alessina's distress at the effect of the electric current on the spirits of that land.

'And then his chickens got bird flu. He'd expanded the flock and he lost them all.'

'That is tough. And he's looking for someone to blame other than bad luck.'

'Looks like it, yes. Trouble is...'

'Yes?'

'There *is* muttering about Alessina. Remember she called back her hedgerow jelly because we found a yew aril in it?'

I did indeed. Lucie continued: 'Mrs Simpkins had already eaten hers and she died a week later.'

'Yes but it was *ten days* later and she had stage four cancer and was under hospice care.'

'Bel, you know these things don't respond to logic,' said Lucie sadly.

She was right. We were facing a genuine witch hunt and I had no idea what to do.

Chapter Five

LUCIE AND I shared a supper of stir-fried vegetables with rice noodles, soy sauce, ginger, garlic and a glug of white wine. The rest of the white wine was also glugged but more directly. I told her everything I could; space-travelling Fiat Pandas, soul retrieval and dead brothers aside, that is. She could handle a possessed bishop because she'd seen possessed children but I barely believe the rest of it myself when I stop and think.

Obviously, I didn't mention the Dean's ghost dog either.

As with most normal human beings, Lucie reacted to the part that affected her first: that I had to go away and would be leaving her either alone or with a stranger. But being the angel she is, she realised that I might be feeling pretty weird myself and that this was a potential problem for Alessina and any local holistic therapists, too.

'*They'll* be okay,' she said wisely. 'Hacked off, certainly, but there are other places for therapists to teach or practice. But Alessina could be in trouble. I don't know how I can protect her if Mr Whipple gets a posse of protest going. I'm afraid Will rather agrees with him,' she added.

'I know,' I said, sadly.

Will was Lucie's boyfriend, a formerly homeless man who had once saved my life and who was now fervently Christian and working towards ordination. He'd frequently tried to tell me off about being friends with Alessina when he'd hoped to be dating me. I'd been relieved when he realised I wasn't his type and I was glad for Lucie… but Will was pretty fundamentalist and that wasn't going to help.

'I suppose she couldn't just protect herself?' Lucie said thoughtfully.

'Indeed she could,' I said. 'But there's also the problem of what's

43

actually behind this anti-witch campaign. There was something rather off around Norris Whipple.'

'Then we pray,' said Lucie simply. 'Do you want to go to the church or shall we do it here?'

Dearest Lucie. Yes, of course we pray. So we did.

Prayer is odd. As God already knows our needs and desires it seems silly sometimes to ask for them in prayer; I'm pretty sure the best prayer in such situations is 'please help me dissolve whatever it is in me that is preventing this happiness/health/financial prosperity.' More complex is the idea of praying for world peace. If, as all the mystics say, God will never interfere with human free will, it's not surprising that prayers to stop conflicts rarely work. Yes, it gets depressing praying for peace and no peace happening but war is very profitable and humans are always getting into conflict of one kind of another, whether it's the tree leaning over your garden fence or the person cutting in front of you at the supermarket. I guess it's true that each one of us has to be at peace before the world itself can be. Frustrating, for sure, but it reminds me of the phrase, '"What can I do? I'm only one person," said seven billion people.'

I heard once that a Swedish journalist got so depressed at having to report on wars that he did a survey where he discovered, to his amazement, that between World War Two and the 1990s, an average of ninety-four per cent of the world had been at peace (at least technically) the whole time. It's probably the same today, though it often doesn't feel like it.

Lucie is young enough not to have lived through too many decades of praying for peace and seeing only temporary phases of calm before another set of animals starts baying at a differently-coloured or alternative-belief country (which probably has oil). And before you say 'animals are better than humans,' yes I agree. Animals may fight and kill but they don't campaign to annihilate all opposition to their ego's beliefs of what is their right. But most humans operate at the animal level with brains that are capable of evil which makes all the difference.

We prayed for guidance and help for the parish. Lucie prayed that I might find some wonderful pathway to follow for the next six months, either here or elsewhere, for strength and help for her to do what was needed and for the perfect (albeit temporary) person to take my place. And we prayed for Alessina's welfare and that of her family.

We prayed in absolute faith because it is easy to trust when you're praying. The secret is not to pick up the problem again, as it was before the prayers, and go on worrying about it. That's the tricky part!

I felt Hero and Lucie's guardian angel, weaving themselves together as we prayed and found myself considering Jesus' words, 'when two or three are gathered together in my name, there I am, among them' (Matthew 18:20).

Silently, I added in my own prayer of some kind of clearer communication with the Dean.

At the final 'Amen,' we opened our eyes and smiled at each other. And for the first time, I perceived Lucie's guardian angel, iridescent in Kingfisher blue and radiating love. For that moment, alone, I knew that the whole parish would be safe in her keeping.

Then my mobile whistled to tell me that a text had come in. I intended to leave it but Lucie touched my hand and said, 'sometimes answers come very quickly.'

I nodded and picked up the phone. Unknown number.

'This is Ben Fairfax. Connie said to contact you about Maisie's funeral. I'm working in Baghdad. Do you WhatsApp?'

'Well?' said Lucie, eyes shining.

'It's certainly an answer to one prayer—at least I think it is,' I said. 'Which is a start!'

It was already 11pm in Iraq so I texted back that we could talk tomorrow; gently turfed Lucie out and went to have an early bath. I know she'd have been happy to have stayed and watched some TV with me but when you spend most of your nights soul retrieving you become somewhat of an old fart in the physical world and I seriously needed some down time. I couldn't remember the last time I went out late at night on Earth—and I had enough adventures without wanting to do anything sociable in the 'real' world.

Jon showed up, as usual around 11pm; I was reading a book

on the sofa and battling a mix of self-pity and overwhelm even despite the fact that last night's visit to the heavens had been so beautiful. I still hadn't discussed the Dean with him or, for that matter, my suspension/sabbatical let alone what last night had meant in terms of our continuing to travel the heavens together. See what I mean about praying and then pulling the problem back to you rather than leaving it in the hands of God?

My brother was always good at disregarding what he called my 'sullens' and when I didn't even get up to greet him, he simply said, 'chop, chop! Things to do; places to go.'

'I have questions,' I said.

'I'd be surprised if you didn't. We can talk on the way.'

'Okay,' I put the bookmark in my old-fashioned physical book and stood up.

Outside was the first surprise of the night. No blue Panda; this one was white.

'Um…?' I said as Jon opened the passenger door for me. He *never* did that. 'What's going on?'

'First, we are tripping into someone else's world,' said Jon, incomprehensibly. 'That is the kind of thing which involves what you'd call a system upgrade.'

'Hence a different illusory car?'

'Hence a different illusory car.'

'So whose world?'

'Xander's,' said Jon. 'You two have something to sort out.'

'You know?'

'Of course I know.' He smiled at me, got behind the driving wheel and leant over to chuck me under the chin like he used to do when I was I child. I hated it then and I wasn't that fond of it now.

'Cheer up,' said Jon. 'It almost certainly *will* happen and, when it does, it'll be absolutely okay.'

'You aren't making any sense at all,' I said peevishly.

'Good,' said my brother, starting the car. 'Making sense is overrated. Buckle up.'

What followed was rather like a version of Charles Dickens' *A Christmas Carol*. No, the Dean wasn't Scrooge (and fortunately neither was I). I'd assumed I'd be meeting with him in present time in the shadow lands where we work but it was that old ineffable thing again; the Holy One has a much wider vision than we humans and despite appearances in our physical brief time-spans on Earth, They appear to know what They are doing. So, instead, I got to experience Xander's past, his present and some of his future ('*They*', by the way, is a perfectly respectable way to refer to the Holy One as the Hebrew Testament is quite clear that they have different aspects—Elohim, Eloah, Yahweh, El Shaddai are only some of the names used for the different faces of the One).

First, I saw the accident where he had the near-death experience which seems to be the life-changing event that lets us work between worlds. In his case, it was a bomb blast in Jerusalem in which his wife was killed and he lost a foot. I'd no idea the Dean had a prosthetic leg but then, why should I? I'd only seen him sitting behind his desk. Fascinatingly, when Jon took me to watch him working with Seraphina, his soul-retrieval companion, I could tell that he had regained the leg.

'That must be both wonderful and confusing,' I said. 'I know people often dream of broken bodies being whole but he's truly experiencing it.' Jon agreed.

The present-day experience showed him with his second wife and made me realise how very stressful it must be to have to keep this kind of work secret.

'He can't tell her?' I said, feeling quite upset as I observed him locking himself into his study each night as his wife went off to bed alone. He always got in with her on his return and they slept together but it was hardly ideal.

Margot's presence didn't help that, either, as he obviously couldn't mention her or even relate to her at home and only a little at the office. I could see how difficult that would be, too.

'You see, he's in a very disciplined habit of dividing the two worlds,' said Jon. 'A lesser man would be unable to do it—and it's not really fair that he has to. However, it has been made clear to him that he is not obliged to do the Work; but he desires to.'

'So, adding me into this world might be the last straw on the camel's back?'

'Exactly. Now can you understand his behaviour?'

'I can. Indeed I can. Selfishly I'm really disappointed because, for me, it would be wonderful to be able to talk and share experiences. But I can see it can't happen. What a shame.'

'Is he happy, do you think? Is his wife happy?'

'Is there anything you can do if they are not?'

'Well… I don't know. I suppose not. Apart from not adding to the pressure.'

'Every little helps!' said Jon with a grin.

The Dean's future was more indistinct and I could only observe it in a kind of sepia: 'There's free will so this might not be the exact outcome,' said Jon. 'But it is by far the most likely one.'

I said nothing to that. The Dean would become a Bishop and then an Archbishop; and an influential one, bringing in a more inclusive form of Christianity—the sort we liberals have been praying for. And a revival of mysticism, too. Marvellous stuff and not easy to achieve in the staid locked-in-the-graven-image of Christianity that pervades today. And to do that, he would need to appear very 'normal' on the path to that level of power. He couldn't afford me.

'So why has he been sent to Devon? And why are we even known to each other?' I asked.

'Because there is one gift he can give you,' said Jon. 'You might never even know about it but it will be done. And it will be important.'

'And that's all I can know?'

'That's all you can know. Remember, you can only be told your own story. This was a benediction so that you didn't rush in where angels fear to tread and push the envelope.'

'Okay. But I can be sad about it.'

'If you want to waste the energy!'

'You know, sometimes you are *very* annoying!'

'We aim to displease,' said Jon with a grin. 'Right, on with the evening's work?'

'Yes, on with the evening's work.'

We joined up with Sam and Callista as usually and, interestingly, given the Dean's experience in Jerusalem, we were there too, this time. Obviously there are generations of souls affected by all the ongoing shenanigans in the Holy Wars which, basically, began when Sarah made Abraham expel Hagar and Ishmael from their tribe, but I had never worked there before. By the magic of spirit I found myself in Muslim garb—just the head-wrap—so that my presence was acceptable to the more orthodox souls we found and helped move through.

'Will there ever be peace here?' I asked Sam as we helped dig through rubble.

'Amazingly, yes!' he said. 'But not yet.'

It was that night that I had the dream that told me of the date when I would die.

Chapter Six

IT REALLY ISN'T something you want to know: the date you will die. Luckily it wasn't *yet* but there's a lot of grieving to be done once you know you aren't going to make old bones. And if the dream was true I was barely going to last through middle age.

I wept. For probably about an hour. It doesn't matter, when it comes to the crunch, if you know for sure that there is an afterlife; that you will see, again, those you have loved and who died; it doesn't matter if you've got more friends on the other side than you have on this, you'll still lose the experience of the physical on this beautiful planet and all the possibilities there, and that hurts.

And who cared that I would have a gravestone that hailed me as an 'apostle of peace'? Okay, obviously I had some important work to do before I shuffled off this mortal coil but what was I to do in the meantime? I was losing my church and my future together and I was going to have to make a lot of decisions, not to mention making a will.

Eventually, as I heard Mrs Tiggy's key in the door, I wiped my eyes and pulled myself together. I managed to be grateful that I am that unusual phenomenon, a beautiful cryer; I can howl and leak for hours without getting swollen eyes or a red face. I have no idea how or why that is but occasionally it's very useful. I did have to tell Mrs Tiggy that I would be taking a sabbatical so if there *were* any signs of my tears that would explain them.

It was school time so Iris and Oliver, the grandchildren from hell, weren't with her today and my heart almost burst with love when I looked into the kitchen at this ferocious-loving, almost circular little body bustling around, putting the kettle on and laying out mugs for our morning tea. I suspect I'll be feeling a lot more of that kind of love now I know the exit plan is in place.

The 'official letter' had also arrived so I picked it up from the kitchen table, where Mrs Tiggy had placed it, told her I had some bad news and asked her if I could have a hug.

Hugging Mrs Tiggy is a complicated matter as she is so short and so round; her face would fit neatly between my breasts but neither of us was entirely keen on that scenario. But, anyway, she didn't feel like a hug today; she was in extra-brisk mode and more likely to chaff me for being a sentimental fool than she was to throw her arms around me. So it was, 'go on with you!' which means 'in your dreams, Sunshine.'

I opened the letter, read it and showed it to her. There were two sheets of paper, the second folded into four, so I disregarded that for the moment and read the primary text. It was just as I expected—I was being released for a three-month sabbatical 'to get some much-needed rest' together with an official review at the end of the period. It was signed by the Dean which was a bit odd as, technically, I thought it should come from the Archdeacon. But it was the Dean I had seen…

'Oh Bella!' said Mrs Tiggy. 'What have you done?'

That woman knows me too well.

'I've been too weird,' I said.

'Well ain't that the truth!' said Mrs Tiggy, opening a packet of chocolate digestives and arranging five on a plate.

I sat down at the table and unfolded the second piece of paper. It was hand-written:

'For hundreds of years, perhaps since the beginning of Creation, a piece of the world has been waiting for your soul to purify and repair it.

And your soul, from the time it was first emanated and conceived, waited above to descend to this world and carry out that mission.

And your footsteps were guided to reach that place.

And you are there now.' Rabbi Tzvi Freeman.

No signature but it simply had to have been written by Xander, the Dean. This was all getting a bit Cosmic, not to mention ineffable.

I gulped and burst into tears.

Mrs Tiggy made the kind of noise that gives a sensitive child in tears a complex for life. It said 'stop being so pathetic' without actually articulating so.

'Come on,' she added. 'It's only three months. You could get yourself a much-needed holiday.'

'*Three* months?' I'd read six months because that's what the Dean had suggested before. But three months was what was written down, so three months it was and three months was much easier to handle.

'So where will you go?' she said. 'Will Lucie take over until you're back?'

'I don't know. I really don't know. I'm not sure they want me back.'

'In which case you get yourself brown and healthy and fight that one when you've had a decent rest,' said Mrs Tiggy. 'You are exhausted, Bella. I've been trying to tell you. It's like you're fitting two lives into one.'

My mobile rang; the WhatsApp signal. It was Ben Fairfax.

'Hello, Bella Ransom,' I said and then held the phone away from my ear as someone commenced bellowing in what sounded like Hebrew. I caught the words *'gamel' 'benzonna'* and something like *'lemower'* but that was about it. However that was, at least, indicative that the bellowing probably wasn't at me.

I put the phone on speaker and laid it down on the table while the rant continued and thoughtfully ate a chocolate digestive.

'What on Earth?' said Mrs Tiggy. 'Why you bother with that internet chat rubbish beats me.'

'It's a relative of Maisie Fenwright's,' I said because I simply wasn't sure about the "husband" bit. 'I think he's somewhere in Iraq. Sounds like he's having trouble with a camel.'

'Well he stopped you from fretting which is something,' said Mrs Tiggy. 'When is Maisie's funeral? I might show up just to make sure.'

'To make sure of what?' I asked but before she could reply, the voice on the phone started to say, 'Hello, hello?'

'Hello,' I replied and couldn't resist showing off a little. 'Having trouble with that son-of-a-bitch camel of yours?'

'It's not mine! Sod the camel. Is that Reverend Amabel Ransom?'

'It is.'

'Right. Well I'm Ben. Maisie's husband. I'm coming over for

the funeral. I'm Israeli so I thought I'd better check if you'd have a problem with that in your church. Are you okay with my saying a few words?'

'At the service? Yes of course. You'll be most welcome. I've been having trouble finding anyone who wanted to speak so actually that would be a relief.' I paused. 'That is, if you have anything remotely positive to say.' I *just* managed not to say anything about the alleged husbanding.

'Ha!' said Ben. 'Yes, she was a character to say the least. Yes, I've do have. But be warned, the family don't like me.'

'May I ask why?' I knew absolutely why…

'Because she and I thought they were a load of freeloading pillocks.' Ben could obviously rival Mrs Tiggy when it came to refusing to mince words.

'And you weren't?' I ventured, bravely.

'Ha!' he went again. I think it was laughter. 'Less so, anyway. So, you're a vicar then. No idea why Maisie would want a vicar at her funeral.'

'I think it's cheaper,' I said, slightly narked. 'She's being buried with her parents so the fees are minimal.'

'And I guess you can't refuse to bury her!'

'I'm not sure why I would want to refuse,' I said somewhat coldly. 'She lived in the parish; her family bought a plot in the churchyard. I'm quite used, by now, to doing services for people who aren't churchgoers.'

'You'd have to be!'

'Anything else I can do for you?' I asked politely. 'Do you know the date and time of the funeral?'

'Next Friday at 11,' he said. 'Drinks at the *Three Hares* afterwards.'

'Are you coming specially? It all seems a bit odd to us people in the sticks.'

'Not really. I do owe the dear crazy old trout but if you're the Amabel Ransom I think you are, I need to talk to you, too, so it's two birds with one stone, if you'll pardon my calling you a bird.'

'Talk to *me?*' Good God, the man used a gerundive correctly! For a moment I felt almost warm towards him.

'You wrote *Mother of God*, didn't you? And you've done some archaeology?'

'Er… yes.'

'Then I need to talk to you. Can you schedule an hour after the drinks after the funeral? It's important.'

Intrigued, I said I supposed I could.

'Good,' said Ben. 'See you then.'

The line went dead.

'So what does some Iraqi heathen want from you then?' asked the not-so-politically-correct Mrs Tiggy.

'I don't know if he is a heathen,' I replied. 'And Abraham came from Iraq, anyway.'

'Abraham was told to *leave* Ur of the Chaldees,' retorted Mrs Tiggy accurately.

'The word "heathen" simply means someone from the countryside,' I countered. 'The etymology comes from "heath dweller." Like the Latin source of "pagan" which originally also meant "country dweller". As you and I are technically country-dwellers we both could be called either.'

Mrs Tiggy sniffed in that wonderfully-expressive way that meant whole paragraphs of justifiable disdain.

'Which reminds me,' I said. 'What do you know of Norris… Oh drat, what was his surname?'

'Norris Whipple?'

'That's the one.'

Mrs Tiggy sniffed again. My years of acquaintance with her told me that this was the depth and range of sniff that outdid your commonplace heathen or pagan.

'A nasty, bitter *little* man.' She said.

Norris wasn't short in stature but I knew exactly what she meant.

'He's coming after Alessina,' I said.

'He would!' said the woman who also deeply disapproved of my friendship with a witch.

'He says there's a groundswell of hostility against her and that she put a spell on his chickens. Mrs Tiggy, I'm worried; if I'm away, I don't know how I can protect her.'

'Well, if she *is* a witch, she can protect herself, surely?' said Mrs Tiggy.

'Remember the witch trials?'

'Yes, but most of those weren't real witches, were they? They were just old women who were inconvenient and probably outspoken about things that shouldn't have been going on anyway.'

Sometimes that redoubtable woman amazes me. She was right on that one for sure.

'Doesn't that make it worse?'

'Of course it does. And yes, I have heard him going on about it and there *are* a few people he's gathered into his nasty snouty little mind-set.'

'Well, you don't approve of Alessina either.'

'Approval is one thing; she don't need my approval. But she don't need the *dis*approval of someone like Norris Whipple. That *could* get nasty.'

'In what way do you think?'

'*You* know,' said Mrs Tiggy, who had never before referred back in any way to the time her grandchildren needed a rather minor exorcism. 'When everyday nastiness gets ramped up into something ugly because it's fed too often and with the wrong stuff. There's no telling how that'll come out but it's never good unless it's nipped in the bud.'

Thoughtfully, I picked up my phone and texted Alessina. I had only a vague hope that she would get it; the mobile signal by her cottage was virtually non-existent and texts could take up to twenty-four hours but I really needed to see her and that would probably mean making an appointment.

Surprisingly, she replied in minutes: 'I'm on my way; I need to see you.'

Serendipity then.

My beautiful friend arrived on the doorstep twenty minutes later. A small part of me was amusedly-indignant that she expected me to drop everything to see her but as there wasn't anything I needed to be doing right then, I couldn't really feed that piece of ego with very much fuel.

We hugged on the doorstep and, to our mutual surprise, we

both began to cry. So we hugged again but deeper, heart to heart, and our tears flowed faster.

"Why are *you* crying?' we asked simultaneously and laughed through the tears. I took her into my office/dining room and shut the door, an indication to Mrs Tiggy that no, we did not want to be asked what we wanted to drink, at least not yet.

'You first,' we said, again simultaneously.

'No you.' Ditto.

'I know when I'm going to die,' I said, just as Alessina said, 'I know when you're going to die.'

'*What?*'

'Okay, okay,' This was me. 'I had a dream that was real. What happened to you?'

'I watched you in your dream,' she said (I did mention she was a witch, didn't I?)

'Go on.'

'I was in the Journey,' said Alessina. The Journey is a shamanic ritual accompanied by drumming, fire and darkness. 'I found myself observing experiencing a lucid dream. My Allies told me this was all real and that it was last night. I saw you, the angels and the marker stone in the church.'

Allies are spirit friends or guides, I believe mostly in animal form; we Christians tend not to know about or have them because we divorced ourselves from the land so many centuries ago but they are real for all that. Darkness frightens us because we don't walk in it with the company and protection of spirit allies. Darkness does not frighten the likes of Alessina.

'And there I was, getting in touch because I wanted to tell you that *you* might be in danger!' I said, which was a bit of an aside given that certain death probably trumps possible persecution.

'Oh *that!*' said Alessina. 'Yes, that's a bit of an issue but let's deal with you first. I realise that this is an incredibly selfish thing to say but I don't want to lose you.'

'I don't want to lose you, either,' I said. 'And I have absolutely no idea what it is that I have to do that, I guess, is going to end my life.

'Oh, and I've been told to take a sabbatical. Which is probably a tactful way of saying "go away and quietly get another job because you're not welcome here."'

'Okay,' said Alessina. 'There's a lot to unpack there. Start at the beginning and tell me everything that you want to tell me.'

She is such a wonderful woman. Note that wording; it's not 'tell me *everything*' but I told her everything anyway.

Alessina has met Jon and knows what I do in the night time and, after fifteen minutes she was completely up to speed.

The first thing she said (apart from 'shall we have a hot drink?') was 'you do know you have free will, don't you? You can choose whether to do the whatever it is that will likely lead to your death. And you can choose at any time.'

'I suspect there's a point of no return,' I said. 'But thank you. The thing is, although ego is absolutely screaming, there's some deeper part of me that is quite certain that there's a path in front that I both want and *need* to follow. That it's absolutely right.'

'Hmmm. Well circumstances are certainly freeing you up to start whatever it is,' said Alessina. 'And Simon the Woodsman's prediction for you before was true so you will be meeting your Anam Cara. I expect he—or she—will have the keys to all this.'

'Or she?' I said, surprised.

'Definitely!' said Alessina. 'A soul mate isn't one you fall in love and live happily ever after with—where's the spiritual growth in that? It's the one person who can inspire you into growing; sometimes it's actually someone you loathe!'

'Oh thanks a bunch,' I grumbled. 'That's all I need.'

'When is Maisie Fenwright's funeral?'

'Friday.'

'Which is five days after the full moon,' said Alessina. 'It could easily be that Ben Fairfax person. Let's face it, he knows what you've written; he's probably wanting to consult you about something.'

'But I don't even remember what I wrote!'

'Then that's your next step, then, isn't it?' said my friend. 'Read the damn book! Find out what it is that you used to know!'

Chapter Seven

IT WAS AN afternoon of both grief and amazement—Walter de la Mare's 'Look thy last on all things lovely; every hour' took on radical new significance. It felt as though the world was alternately grey (when I felt depressed or afraid) and incredibly bright when I allowed myself to look afresh at all the beauty around me. I moved through parish duties automatically and, slowly and steadily, there came a deep conviction that stepping out of this job, at least for a time, would be a deep refreshment. I wouldn't even be able to feel all that guilty as it hadn't been my decision. After all, if was going to lose my life, I'd better make sure that I lived it as well as I could.

I still had concerns for Alessina's safety but she reassured me she could take care of herself. And nothing *had* actually happened apart from some posturing, after all.

For supper, I cooked myself gnocchi with roasted vegetables and goats cheese, opened a bottle of shiraz, picked up one of my author copies of *Mother of God,* got over myself about the appalling title and began to read.

It was a fairly interesting book about the Hebrew First Temple. Even though I'd written it myself, I didn't remember much about it (I suppose when I do die, I'll get my memory back—for all the good that will do me then!) but there were echoes in there which were familiar.

I could see pretty soon why it was such a popular/unpopular book, depending on how orthodox a faith you held, as it focused on worship of the Divine Feminine in ancient days and how that used to be part of the story for the pre-Moses generations of the Hebrews, too. It looked as though Mosaic law and the Yahwist texts (as opposed to the earlier Elohist texts) were the start of what we now know as the Patriarchy.

By chapter five, despite finding the author's writing style rather dense, I was hooked. Did I really know all this stuff? I must have done. The actual focus of the whole thing was how the stories of the Virgin Mary and Mary Magdalene were both metaphors for the Goddess worship of the ancient days. I had even dared posit that the coming of Jesus and early Christianity were an attempt to return to the teachings of the First Temple, which fell in the sixth century BCE. I bet that went down like a lead balloon at Lambeth Palace.

The Goddess was thrown out of that temple when King Josiah's high priest conveniently found two books of the law in the Holy of Holies and the whole edifice was razed to the ground to be rebuilt according to the law. From then on, worship *had* to be in the temple under the aegis of the priestly class; before, it had often taken place in nature and trees were honoured as representatives of the Goddess.

It's all hidden in plain sight in the Hebrew Bible if you know what you're looking for and, by the time Jon showed up, I was knee-deep in Bible translation software on my laptop, checking out the references I had used.

I still don't know how I can physically hug the ghost of my brother but I can and it's such a relief. He knew, of course, just as Alessina had, as it would appear that secrets were not much of an option in the heavens.

'Let's just go somewhere to talk,' said Jon. 'There are big changes for all of us ahead; they're all in the nature of things but change is always difficult when you've still got a human ego attached.'

'Do you still have a human ego?'

'Yes, to a certain extent; I've been experiencing my identity from my life in order to work with you but once that's finished, I can move onward and upwards and start considering what's next for my soul; there's more and different work to do. And, frankly, Bel, human soul-seekers get burnt out after a year or two. We have to retire you before you end up going bonkers. Xander will be retired pretty soon, too.'

'Does that mean he'll die as well?'

'No, his destiny is different. But he can't go on much longer doing two jobs at once.'

'Because he has an important job to do down here?'

'As do you. But Bel, you *do* have free will. This task you've accepted—and yes, it does sound a bit like *Mission Impossible* doesn't it?—can be turned down. You could simply return to being a country rector.'

'Only if my memory of what we've been doing was erased,' I said. 'It would be like losing half my life otherwise.'

'There is that,' said Jon.

'Would I die at the same time whether I did the work or not?'

'No, you'd have a longer life here.'

'With every day wondering what I *could* have done to become an apostle of peace—whatever that means.'

'Yes. And, having moved on, you wouldn't see me—or Marcus—or Sam or Callista of course, again. There's another thing, Bel…'

'Yes?'

'You've been on borrowed time ever since that first car accident. You died, remember? Such severe head injuries carry physical echoes, as you know. You still have regular check-ups at the hospital so they can monitor you. It's quite likely you would never have made old bones. That wasn't part of the destiny for either of us this time.

'And also, remember, there are hundreds of thousands of people right now who are reeling from a terminal diagnosis. Most of them have no abiding faith in a life after death—and many believe there is nothing at all to come. You at least know that there is more; there are souls who love you deeply on the other side, not to mention a pale-coloured hound who would love to visit you regularly.'

'I do miss her,' I said. Seraphim, the inaccurately-named foxhound who had become my ghost-dog until I helped her free her original Earth-bound master, had gone back to the heavens with him. She would 'dry' my legs with her tongue when I got out of the bath and slept on my bed. Even a ghost hound makes a house feel less empty. And I was half in love with Marcus the heavenly dog wrangler, too…

'You do have to make a decision as to whether you are willing to do this work,' said Jon. 'It's that old Goethe quotation that the moment one definitely commits oneself, then Providence moves as well. Nothing can happen until you make the decision.'

'I thought I had,' I said, forbearing to correct him about the quotation which was, in fact, from William Hutchinson Murray, in his 1951 book *The Scottish Himalayan Expedition*. What do they teach them in these heavenly schools?

'Well, you're havering.'

'No, grieving, not havering. I'm on for the adventure and even though I can't see myself as an apostle of peace the world certainly needs one and I'm willing to do my best.'

'Okay,' said Jon. 'In which case, I am authorised to take you somewhere tonight to view the past. It's one of those "need to know basis" visits and once you've been, there'll be no turning back. Is that clear?'

'Very clear. Will it show me what I have to do?'

'Indirectly. But it will give you the impetus.'

'Well, I guess that's something.'

We were in the white Panda again that night and the journey seemed to involve circling the Earth anti-clockwise at incredible speed a dozen times.'

'Are we going back in time?'

'Yes, about three thousand years.'

'Wow!'

We landed just before sunrise in what looked like some part of the Middle East, outside what appeared to be a walled temple complex. It was in a valley with a town of rather cluttered flat-roofed houses rising up the nearby hillside and another, newer temple on the summit.

Memory stirred—not the old, lost memories, but something from the book I had just been reading.

'Oh my God,' I said as we got out of the car. 'Is this the Hebrew First Temple?'

'Indeed it is,' said Jon. 'And on that hill is the Temple of Baal.'

'Oh can we go inside this one?' I was thrilled. 'Oh please!

'But—hang on—isn't that what we now call the Temple Mount? A temple of *Baal?*'

'Yes, and Baal's wife is Asherah which is similar to the name of the Goddess-energy in this temple here so that's leading to a lot of confusion—one reason why this original temple is losing its power and about to corrupt itself. You see, Baal demands human sacrifice and, as long as that's of an enemy, everyone thinks it's rather fun so he is growing more and more popular.'

'Rather *fun?*'

'Well yes. It's the worst part of human nature. People have always loved to view public executions.'

'But not here,' I looked at the temple in front of us.

'Not here—yet. But soon King Manasseh will sacrifice the eldest son he wants to get rid of and the whole temple will come down.'

'Oh yes, I was just reading about that today. His grandson, King Josiah's high priest, will find the books of the Law in the Holy of Holies and the whole Mosaic era begins. The end of any hope of Matriarchy. Oh Jon it hasn't happened yet! This is so exciting!'

'Come on then; we are ghosts here so we can go in but we still need to be respectful.'

'Of course!'

Don't let anyone tell you that walking through walls is pleasant because it isn't. It feels like eating dirty gravel with your skin. But the temple doors were closed so we had little alternative. Inside, women with besom brooms were sweeping the floors of the outer court which was beautifully decorated with palisades, fountains and well-tended flowering bushes. Oh, the colours! When archaeologists dig up old ruins, they are usually bare stone with just tiny traces of the original paint and, of course, the British Reformation destroyed much of the bright beauty of our old Catholic churches so we're not used to radiant colour in places of worship. But this! Blues and reds and greens and yellows and exquisitely-carved pergolas with wooden benches for people to rest out of the sun.

I ran around like a child, swathed in delight—and this was just the outer court; the one where all visitors could go. One thing that fascinated me in particular was the water course in the courtyard. Clear fresh water flowed, seemingly from the heart of the temple. There was no roof and the afternoon sun created long shadows everywhere.

Next, we went through to what, in the Second Temple, would be called *The Court of the Women* but here, it was simply a place for all believers and their families. As women were part of the whole temple worship, there was no need to segregate them. Thoughts differ on whether the women of the Second Temple were able to look over into the Court of the Men, as in modern-day orthodox synagogues, or whether they were kept completely apart. By the time of the Second Temple they certainly became excluded. Again, the stream flowed from the centre through the entire court.

As the First Temple had no decreed animal sacrifices, there was no separate entrance for bringing the larger creatures in or collection or distribution points for the sacrificed meats and the next court—which was roofed and lit only with flaming sconces which showed richly-painted walls and a glittering mosaic floor— was for both priests and priestesses instead of being, basically, a charnel house. Some of the people were already present, bringing in bread and wine which were the traditional temple offerings— to be taken into the Holy of Holies to be sanctified before being brought out and shared around. No one knows if only the officials ate the blessed food or if it went out to the people themselves; I'd like to think the latter but given religion's propensity to value status, it probably wasn't so.

Beyond these courts was the shrine of the Holy of Holies. Either side of it was a great pillar and my heart sang when I saw that the one on the left (the feminine) was, indeed, black and the one on the right (masculine) was white. The Second Temple called them the pillars of Boaz and Jachin as only the masculine was honoured there.

I paused but Jon walked straight in so, in what I realise is a horrible irony, I crossed myself and followed, my heart in my mouth.

Oh my God. It was like a Tardis. I have no idea how it was lit but I could see quite clearly. A wide corridor contained beautifully-carved tables, including one containing the exquisite golden jar of anointing oil, other golden ornaments, silken tapestries depicting the Tree of Life and hangings of fur and of scarlet, purple, blue and white. In the centre was a small, deep pool with what looked like a spring bubbling up from underground. This must be the source of the stream running throughout the temple.

And there were *ten* menorot along the sides of the room with what was presumably the great, original, one veiled at the far end. Something behind that veil appeared to move and shine; you couldn't look that hard because it was too bright for human eyes

I actually felt quite faint and had to take Jon's hand to steady myself. He looked down at me with a loving smile and said, 'Quite a sight, isn't it?'

I couldn't answer him; my mind was blown.

Once I'd stared my fill at what I *could* look at, I realised, much to my surprise, that the seven-branched candlesticks were somewhat differently shaped from the carving showing the menorah being paraded in Rome after being looted from the Second Temple. They had straight arms, were more delicate and I could smell the scent of burning oil around the wicks in their seven ornate cups.

'I can smell them!' I said (what prosaic words when situated in such a paradise!) 'But we're ghosts; there shouldn't be scent.'

'Did you not smell the flowers in the outer courts?' said Jon.

'Obviously not. How strange.'

'Ineffable,' said Jon knowledgeably and I hit him in the ribs. 'And that's no kind of behaviour in this kind of place, young lady!'

'Sorry.' And I was. Tentatively, I walked closer to the Ark of the Covenant, that incredible icon of Jewish faith and history and, with no one to stop me and a child's fascination and absolutely no inkling of what might be sacrilegious, wrong or simply unwise to do, I touched a golden wing on one of the cherubim on the Ark.

It felt soft, like real feathers. Soft and icy cold. So cold it felt as though it freeze-burnt the tip of my fingers and I jumped. Then the angel itself moved; it was a living Being, and it looked at me with eyes of fire. Words of the equivalent of And you are...? Came into my head.

'Sorry,' I muttered

And you are? Was repeated. It was a genuine question.

'I'm Bella Ransom,' I stuttered.

You are one who will uncover the heart. It was a statement, not a question.

'Um… I don't know.'

Then BECOME one who uncovers the heart. That was very definitely an order.

'Erm… yes.' I bowed and the cherub bowed back. Then it was still again.

'Oh wow,' I said to John, who was standing behind me, smiling.

'Do you think I can touch one of the menorot?'

'I think you can do anything you want; do you *want* to touch a menorah?'

'Oh yes.'

'Well take care then. As you can see, these are living icons.'

Not only icons.

I reached out and touched one magnificent golden candlestick. The world began to swirl in a spectrum of colour that I could taste and hear and smell and I was spinning in a whirlwind of fire and dumped unceremoniously into another dimension.

Chapter Eight

I LANDED, IF that's the right word, in a vast chamber of wispy-twinkling light which included both delicate music and delicious scent experienced in the very depths of my spirit body. It took a moment or two to focus my sight; everything seemed vague and flowing but, as I picked myself up from a surprisingly soft floor, I found myself before an image of the very same menorah that I had touched—but one made up purely from light. As I looked at it, it shifted form like a fluent melody, to become first the Greek Orthodox cross with its three bars, then a triple version of the Islamic crescent moon and star, a weaving of the OM sign and then a series of sigils which I didn't recognise and back to the menorah again.

I could have watched it for hours; so very beautiful a weave of symbols, simultaneously diverse and one.

The twinkling formulated itself into seven silvery souls standing around the menorah of light. I felt them simultaneously speak a welcome and then one of them stepped forward and began to formulate itself into an image. She—it presented as a She—flowed through what I could only intuit to be a series of incarnations until it settled on one: a woman with skin, eyes and hair the same colour as mine. Her hair was plaited and coiled around a beautiful diadem of soft gold and precious stones.

As she coalesced we fell, together, in a sickening dive through to yet another dimension and I found myself on my hands and knees on a mosaiced floor in front of her throne, dizzy and gasping and suddenly terrified. My hand, where I had touched the menorah, now stung with burning but that was the least of my problems.

She was a queen; there could be no doubt about that; her face was lined and fierce and her power felt absolute. The colours and scents around her throne were so bright as to make it impossible to look. I had no idea where or *when* I was or who she might be. Before I could fully focus, she addressed me in old Hebrew.

And I understood her.

I know Hebrew but would have said I was pretty out of touch with the ancient version. I didn't have a Douglas Adams babel fish but something was making sure I could remember all I had learnt and could easily comprehend her.

'Sit, child,' she said.

I knelt instead. She nodded, recognising that as respect. Respect was appropriate.

'Have you come to aid us?' she asked.

I looked up. I knew that looking kings and queens in the eyes was not recommended in ancient days but I couldn't help it. She certainly wasn't young, probably about my own age, but she looked much older. People didn't live that long in Biblical times and she looked very much a Biblical queen. I thought her terrifying, breathtakingly beautiful and incredibly sad.

Then she smiled, all shadows retreated and her face lit up.

'Sit,' she said again.

I readjusted myself and sat.

'Your Majesty,' I said, bowing my head.

'You understand me?' She was looking slightly confused and I remembered that 'Majesty' was a later fashion in addressing royalty.

'I can, Lady.'

'Good. I repeat my question: have you come to aid us?'

'I don't know,' I said, honestly. 'I hope so. I touched a menorah in the temple…'

'Ah,' she sighed. 'Then you *have* been sent. You are the last of the three. Much is required of you for the others failed.'

'The last of the three? The others?'

'There are three allotted by the Holy One for any great task so that if one or even two fail, the third may still be sent forth.'

I puffed up my cheeks and blew in a *pffft* sound. No pressure then.

'My Lady, do you know what it is I must do to help you? For I have not been informed.' My words all came out in the same language as hers; respectful and formal.

'You must find me,' she said with a smile. 'Find me in the time in which you now live, for that will lead you to the temple whence you came today. Only when you have found that place is there hope for peace amongst my peoples.'

'How do I find it, Lady?'

She laughed. 'Do not ask! You are chosen to search. All I can tell you is that the Temple my son built was set on running water. I cannot tell if that water still runs but I do know that the temple that Ezra built was *not* on running water.'

'Your son, Lady?'

'The King. Solomon,' she said.

So this was Queen Bathsheba, David's wife. The Lady who crowned her son and sat on his right when he ruled, as was the custom then. The Queen was the king's mother, not his wife, until death.

'Madam. I will do my best,' I said.

'You will do more; you will succeed,' she said. 'Even so, it may not be enough. A whole resurrection is needed for humanity but it will begin the process at the level your people can now perceive.

'It is agreed then. Your angel may take you now.'

That was indeed a dismissal. For the first time that day, I felt Hero's presence. She wrapped her wings around me as I stood up and bowed to the Lady and then the swirling began again.

I truly thought I would be sick but I landed, safe in the soft wings, back in the temple.

'Ah,' said Jon. 'Must say, that's a bit of a relief.'

'I met Bathsheba,' I gibbered. 'I spoke with her. I have to find her grave. How do I do that?'

'Well, I expect you'll be shown a path,' said Jon. 'They wouldn't bring you this far if you were going to be left dithering, would they? 'I suspect you've got enough for the moment. Patience is a virtue, remember?'

'God I used to hate it when you said that!'

'And do you hate it now?'

'I'm not very good with hate any more,' I confessed.

'Good,' said Jon. 'Now I'll take you home.'

So he did.

Before I went to bed that night, I looked out at the bright full moon with clouds scudding across it. My Anam Cara was on his way; my destiny was beginning to unfold.

My last vicarly duty before suspension—sorry, *sabbatical*—was to be Maisie Fenwright's funeral and most of my time in between was helping Lucie prepare to take on the full yoke of service. As is so frequent nowadays, she was going to be left to sink or swim— no available supervising priests right now or, at least, none who would be willing to come to a place where the incumbent might still be living.

'But Will can help me!' she said with shining eyes. Yes he would love to do that and, if he had any influence, it meant my lovely relaxed church would be stepping up into the evangelical world. I'd been so grateful to Will when he saved me but nowadays I was more than wary. I'd had a dream/experience/parallel universe experience with Will back when he wanted us to be a couple and that had put me on my guard. But he seemed to be making Lucie happy and I couldn't begrudge her all the help she could get.

There'd been another meeting with the Parish Council, obviously, where I had to bite my tongue while being berated for being so selfish as to leave everyone in the parish in the lurch while simultaneously being informed that it had been obvious for some time that I wasn't firing on all cylinders and that Lucie was an absolute treasure. Bless her, she fired up in my defence and because she is just so beautiful, they apologised and wished me well, although I expect there was also some relief that we wouldn't have to be speaking again for quite some while.

Lucie and I were having supper together two days before Maisie's funeral when the doorbell went. It's fair to say that nowadays nobody knows what time people have their supper and I guessed the caller must be one of those strange folk who eat at 6pm—or even stranger—after 8.30pm. We were halfway through rigatoni with roasted leeks, peppers and tomatoes in chili-infused olive oil with garlic and chunks of feta and there *wasn't* going to be enough for a guest.

I sighed but shook my head when Lucie offered to go in my

place. If you knock on the vicar's door in the evening, I said, the odds are you are looking for the vicar. Lovely, talented and delightful though my assistant was, it wasn't her they were seeking.

'Unless, of course, they knocked on my door first,' said Lucie, cheekily, which made me snort with laughter. God, I can be arrogant sometimes!

It was the Dean. He was in mufti and had a cloche hat on his head so I honestly didn't recognise him for a minute.

'I need your help,' he said.

'Okay.'

'Please,' he said.

'Okay,' I said again. 'I'm just finishing supper. Do you want to come in?'

Then he bit me. And I mean *bit* me. Of course it wasn't the Dean that bit, it was what he was carrying with him. Something Jesus might have called a demon and I suspect that Jesus would have been right.

'*Shit!*' I said. Because it hurt; it was like being stabbed by a knitting needle in all the main nerve ganglia.

Xander held his arms out towards me. 'I'm sorry,' he said. And he was weeping now. 'I'm so sorry. I didn't know what to do. Can you help? What do we do?'

'*LUCIE!*' I bellowed, while I still had time. 'Get Alessina. *Don't* come to the front door. *Don't* come and look at me. I mean it! Go out the back and *get Alessina NOW*'

Did she obey me? Did she hell. We never do, do we? And I bet I wouldn't have, either. She came to see what on Earth was going on. So it bit her as well. Poor Lucie; she'd been bitten before without realising it; this time she knew and she screamed and fell. Twice bitten would be a lot worse than once and I had to act. Somehow I still had time although I could feel darkness filling me like mud slowing my blood.

'Church. NOW' I hissed, pulling Xander through the house. And as we staggered together through the French windows to cross the garden into the churchyard, a single bee buzzed by my head.

The bees! Of course. I'd completely forgotten. 'Fetch Alessina!' I said to it. 'Go now.

'And...' It was bees who saved Lucie before. It was worth a try. I staggered back and opened the French windows again. 'Help her!' I said.

I'd confused the bee. Not surprising; I was confusing myself. But I had given it two separate orders.

'Sorry,' I said, somewhat pointlessly because bees don't tend to apologise much or even recognise what an apology is meant to mean. 'Reset: please go to the hive; send bees to fetch Alessina and send other bees to help Lucie.' If they did, it meant she'd be stung to buggery but strangely, demons can't handle bee stings and have to head off somewhere else—at least, they did last time the poor girl was possessed. Demons don't vanish; energy cannot be destroyed, only changed, as the scientists say, but they really like being stung even less than humans do.

'Thank you,' I added because it's only polite.

Half-way to the church and still pretty much dragging the Dean, I remembered that it would be locked and I didn't have the key. But this church is an entity of its own and it had unlocked itself for me before. I could only hope (because when you've been bitten it's fucking hard to pray) that Ariel, the church angel, had managed to sort something.

She had. We staggered in and I called 'Sanctuary, sanctuary, SANCTUARY' as we did.

Now, I have to admit that it's foolish to think that God is in churches and not anywhere else. The Divine is everywhere, permeating everything, but this space was where I said communion, where people had prayed for centuries and where the angelic presence was strong. And the church had experience of demonic energy and, if anything could help this particular biting thing, I would find it here.

I dragged the Dean up the nave and, bless her, Ariel opened the rood doors for us so we collapsed together against the altar. Xander now was muttering, 'sanctuary, sanctuary' too and I had, finally, a moment to assess what was going on inside and around us.

There was something inside me that was trying to think for me. We all have those negative voices in our head (don't we? I hope it's not just me) but this wasn't me; it was a parasite trying to feed on all my bad thoughts; different from the other demons I'd encountered but then, again, this was the first time that any of them had managed to get inside of me. That's not because I'm holier than thou, by the way, it's because they latch onto bad thoughts and memories and my having lost most of my memory it had been hard for them to get a grip on me. But obviously that was changing.

There was a moment of relief that it wasn't feeling all that bad but that was followed by an angelic message of awareness that it would strengthen as it ate my thoughts and soon it would begin to eat me.

'Oh God, that's better,' said the Dean. I guess I'd better start calling him Xander as it looked as if we were going to get to know each other—and each other's demons as well.

Demon in hitchhiker, said Hero in my head.

'What?'

Human soul who refused to go at death. Now infested. Needs living human for life force.

'Is that better or worse than "just" a demon?'

The answer was along the lines of *Meh!*

'Who are you talking to?' said Xander/the Dean.

'Oh sorry. Angels. Can't you perceive them?'

'No, I'm afraid not.'

'Is his an infected hitchhiker too?' I asked.

Yes. They are legion.

'Oh shit. What do we do?'

Identify hitchhikers. Create a path. A bridge to heavens. Invite guardians to unite soul. Leave demons behind.

'O… kay…'

'Wait a minute,' I said to Xander. 'Just working something out.'

'But it's gone!'

'Has it? Mine hasn't.'

I could tell that he wasn't on board; he obviously felt much better but, as always, there was more work to do than just turning up in a church and yelling 'Sanctuary!' That could help but every demonic-type little bugger is adept at hiding and it would appear that hitchhikers might be too.

'Can you help?' I said to both Ariel and Hero.

Help, yes. Bring Rus-El, too. Summon him.

Rus-El was the generic name for a series of angels which had been created to protect me once I became so weird. Every single one of them so far had been destroyed in their duty but they still kept turning up.

'Rus-El!' I called.

A red light crashed into the lady chapel next to us.

Oops it said as it knocked over a candlestick and the picture of the virgin toppled forward onto the altar. I never knew angels went *oops*. I didn't know that angels could be clumsy.

It emerged through the wooden screen and, despite not having feet, trod on Xander who, fortunately, didn't notice.

This version of Rus-El was chunky and red and armoured, pretty much humanoid as before but, this time, definitely presenting as female. That was a first.

Go invisible was her first command—and it *was* a command, not an instruction.

Once, at the beginning, the original Rus-El had given me the powers of temporary invisibility. Through an angelic-human misunderstanding I activated the power by saying (or thinking) the words 'Good grief!' so I said that.

I was still holding on to Xander but he didn't notice any change so I didn't know if it had worked.

Yes, working. All incarnate you are touching also.

And—weirdly (but that is now a very normal word)—we appeared to be invisible to the hitchhikers, too, because I could now perceive them; probably six grey spirits wafting around where we still were but disconnected. Within them was something very shiny and very grey and very, very nasty with an awful lot of teeth. In those teeth hung what looked like shreds of bloody skin.

Now, said Rus-El who appeared to be separating them out and corralling them in a kind of cosmic lasso-thingy-wotsit. Then she, Ariel, Hero and Xander's guardian, too, began to sing.

It was an eerie, silvery song and it built an eerie silvery bridge in the very air that I could somehow perceive stretched to infinity. And another song came back to us as beings of light appeared, moving down the bridge towards us and singing both in contrast and in harmony.

Speak to send the hitchhikers I heard in my head. Xander was trying to speak, too, but, somewhat roughly, I put my hand over his mouth; hissed 'trust me!' and spoke to the wisp of grey.

'This is the highway to heaven,' I said. 'Here are your guardian angels to take you home. All you have to do is touch the bridge and you are free. I send you back to the Source to be healed and transmuted. Go!' It seemed to make sense at the time.

Five of them flowed towards and then onto the bridge and I sensed joy in the reunion and they and their angels retreated upwards. The fifth, which now carried the shiny thing, held back; there was tussling as the demon held it. The remaining angel on the bridge called to it.

Then Rus-El ended her part in the singing and produced a very large and sharp three-pronged sword with which she stabbed the demon and pulled it out as though she was de-shelling a snail.

With what appeared to be a gasp of relief, the last shadow smoked itself to the bridge and its angel and they were gone. The bridge itself seemed to fold up and vanish and we were left with Rus-El and the demon in a stand-off.

It wasn't so much a fight, despite that impressive trident, as it was a series of energetic communications. Rus-El, to my surprise, was radiating a kind of deep loving powerful *No* rather than actually attacking. The demon, on the other hand, was absolutely on the attack. But it was chaotic; it didn't have any form of focus; it had obviously been relying on some kind of form in the humans' etheric for any kind of structure. Rus-El was, basically, rounding it up.

'What the hell's going on?' said Xander.

'What can you see?'

'Sod all but I know something's happening.'

'Okay, well we were infested with lost souls and there was a demon attached to them. My guardian and the angel of the church have helped me sort the former and there's a protective angel currently doing what she can to sort the latter.'

'I think you are amazing,' said the Dean, and kissed me.

Chapter Nine

IT ISN'T POLITE to laugh when someone kisses you but when you're so surprised you don't close your eyes and therefore see three angels staring at you and going the celestial equivalent of *WTF?* It's fairly unavoidable.

Three angels because I now saw the Dean's own guardian clearly. Rus-El was still busy…

'Um… sorry,' I said, being a middle-aged woman and therefore part of a species and generation which was trained to apologise even when submitted to what safeguarding would now call a sexual assault, *WTF?* really should have been my reaction too.

Possibly laughter wasn't entirely appropriate either.

'Sorry!' said the Dean (I simply *can't* seem to call him Xander). 'Sorry! *So* sorry. It was the heat of the moment and I do think you're amazing.'

'You're married,' I said somewhat snarkily, pushing him away. 'And we're not even out of this mess yet.' The last bit was irrelevant but very, very accurate. You see, with all that had been going on at the high altar, I had forgotten about Lucie, who was now standing at the church door—with three of the parish council.

Had they seen the kiss? No, because we were invisible. At least we were until I pushed the Dean who suddenly *became* visible.

Oops.

Lucie, who hadn't met the new Dean, said 'Who are you?' to the strange man sitting up against the high altar in her church.

He might have replied but then, right on dramatic cue, the bees arrived; a whole swarm diving in through the open doorway behind Lucie, Colin, Diana and David, all of whom shrieked and ducked. Lucie screamed the loudest. She was probably being stung.

Alessina strode behind them like a beautiful avenging angel, a bottle of her legendary elderflower champagne Holy Water in one hand and a netted bee hat in the other.

The bees ignored everyone but Rus-El and the demon although the screaming didn't stop. I suspect the demon was screaming, too.

Because Alessina is a witch, she could see me and what's more she could tell I was invisible (that sentence makes sense; it just doesn't sound as if it does).

She beckoned and tipped her head to suggest I left the scene. I'm not exactly proud of it but that's exactly what I did. I got up, walked around everyone and out of the church. Behind me, I heard Alessina's voice, authoritative and loud:

'Don't panic. I will gather up the bees and take them away. Just leave the church quietly.'

Whether they obeyed her, I don't know. I trotted back across the churchyard, into my back garden and back inside through the wisteria-bathed French windows, bumping into a strange man in tweeds who was pondering my bookshelves.

'Um,' I said because it had been quite a tiring day and I was fast running out of energy. He heard me and turned but of course I was sodding invisible, wasn't I? (it usually lasted about half an hour for each 'good grief').

'Are you a ghost?' he said.

'What?'

'I heard a voice and I can perceive that someone's there,' he said. 'Are you a ghost?'

'Er, no.'

'Then I presume you are Reverend Doctor Phaedra Amabel Velvet Ransom?'

'Um, yes. But how do you know all my weird names?'

'I'm Ben Fairfax,' he said. 'We knew each other briefly when you were doing your PhD.'

'You can see me?' I said rather confused. I had no memory of either PhD (and I still can't work out why I would have wanted *two!*) and no idea why I would have revealed all my appalling names to this man but that wasn't my priority right now.

'Obviously,' said the man, dryly. 'Though what you are up to is rather beyond me. Are you generally this ethereal nowadays?'

'Er, no. I'm usually quite normal.'

'That I sincerely doubt,' said Ben. 'By the way, you are staring.'

I was; I admit it. It was the nose. And the clothes. But the nose...

It's a ridiculous, insulting and inaccurate ethnic stereotype that Jewish folk have large, hooked noses but this man had a corker. It wasn't so much a nose on a face than a face on a nose. The tweeds didn't help; they made him look as though he'd come directly from a Downton Abbey pheasant shoot. Not only did he wear tweeds, he had a yellow waistcoat and he even had a monocle hanging on a ribbon round his neck. He raised the glass and stared back at me through it. He appeared to have escaped from the nineteenth century although he had, mercifully, spared me the vision of plus fours.

'I'm afraid I don't remember you,' I said. 'Did we know each other well?'

'Quite well,' he said. 'But we lost touch very swiftly.' His voice was deep, velvety even. You can fall in love with a voice like that although you would still have to get over the clothing and the nose.

'Ah,' I said. 'How did you get in here?'

'I simply followed three other people who seemed to think that they had the right of entry. Were they incorrect?'

'It's a moot point.' I sighed. 'Do synagogues have the equivalent of a parish council?'

'I wouldn't know. Who told you I was Jewish?'

'You did. On the phone. You thought I might object to my having you speak in the church.'

'So I did,' he said, remembering. 'Do you have five minutes now? Or are you currently in the process of fading away?'

'You seem to be remarkably pragmatic about this.'

'Yes,' he said. 'And you seem to be remarkably transparent.'

'That won't last; it's only a maximum of thirty minutes. But while it *is* lasting, do you think we could go for a walk because there's a bit of a ruckus at the church which will almost certainly boil over into this house and I'd rather not manifest in the middle of it.'

'Curiouser and curiouser,' said Ben. 'Lead the way, Bathsheba.'
I stopped dead. '*What* did you call me?'

'I called you Bathsheba; you do know who Bathsheba was?'

'Of course I do! But I fail to see the significance.'

'*Go out, O daughters of Zion, and look upon King Solomon, with the crown with which his mother crowned him on the day of his wedding,*' he quoted.

'Song of Solomon,' I shot back. 'But again…'

'All will become clear,' he said. 'Or maybe not. Who knows? Would you care to lead the way?'

The sound of voices could now be heard from the garden.

'Yes—follow me,' I said, making a sharp exit through the front door and out into the lane.

I live on the edge of the village so the choice was to turn right towards the village shop, the church hall and a row of houses with possibly twitching curtains or left along the road with a verge frothing with wildflowers and the risk of being flattened by a tractor. That way, within a hundred yards, there was a footpath which wound back around the church and onto the moor and it hadn't rained for a whole forty-eight hours so it might just be passable. After swiftly assessing my visitor's footwear—brogues—I chose the left.

We walked silently in single file with me leading the way until the stile that led to the footpath where, to my surprise, he stepped ahead of me and over. It was only when he offered me his hand to help me step down from the stile that I realised that he was being a gentleman.

'Thank you,' I said. 'Are you sure you belong in the twenty-first century?'

He barked a laugh. 'Frankly? No!'

'And yet you married Maisie online…' I let that one hang to see if he would take the bait. He didn't.

We wove our way around the muddiest bit, soon finding ourselves on a path wide enough for two and overhung with elderflowers.

'Just in case you are interested, you are fully visible now,' said Ben. He looked me up and down with the monocle again. It was incredibly disconcerting.

'Why do you use that?' I asked.

'Because it disconcerts people,' he said. 'People frequently need to be disconcerted, in my experience. And, strangely, because it helps me to see more clearly. I have astigmatism in one eye. However, in fact, it is, of course, a magical tool which ensures I can see invisible things.'

'Really?'

'No.'

'And why do you want to disconcert me?'

'Just habit, I suppose.'

We walked on.

'So…?' I said. 'What is it you want to talk to me about that will only take five minutes?'

'Oh that's quite simple. I need your help to rediscover the First Temple in Jerusalem,' he said. 'I'm pretty sure I've found the location but I've been told that we should do it together.

'There are seven of us,' he added. 'Mo and Ali are Muslim, Jakob, Isa and Asher are Jewish agnostics, Malin is Bahai and God knows what Delyth is. You're Christian, of course. But that's not the main reason.'

'Which is?' I could feel my heart swelling with a strange joy while my brain tried the 'What the hell? Don't be stupid! The man is mad' kind of dance that the ego just loves to throw at anything that might offer an adventure.

'It's your job,' he said, turning to look at me without brandishing a monocle. Eyes met eyes. His were dark brown and seemingly clear of any devilment. 'It is our destiny.'

'Okay,' I stopped short. 'Who are you really and what's going on?'

'I'm exactly who I say I am with the additional—and I believe mutual—ability to perceive slightly more than your average Joe,' said Ben, continuing to walk. 'For example, your guardian angel is currently clearer than you are; it projects a feminine appearance with dark hair and it is perfectly happy with my guardian.'

True, said Hero.

Why the fuck can't I see his then? I asked.

Permissions, said Hero.

Did I give him permission to see you?
No, I did.
Oh great. So his guardian hasn't given me permission.
No reply. Angels don't bother with the bleedin' obvious.

'And,' Ben went on, as I trotted after him. 'To quote Martin Luther King junior, "I have a dream." It may be a particularly stupid dream but I have always believed that finding the First Temple might just assist in the peace process.'

'You mean because it wasn't in the same place as the Second Temple?'

'Exactly. I didn't know until I read your book that the First Temple was located on living water. It makes sense, of course and, as far as I can tell, there had never been natural flowing water at the site of what is now the Dome of the Rock. And why on Earth *would* they build the Second Temple on the desecrated and unhallowed ground of the despised first?'

'It's not my research,' I said hastily. 'It was originally Dr Margaret Barker's research and she built her work on *The Temples that Jerusalem Forgot* by Ernest L. Martin. I know he's long gone but why aren't you approaching Dr. Barker? And if we actually found that temple, you think the two-state concept could work?'

Now it was Ben's turn to stop.

'Frankly? No,' he said. 'I have very little hope for peace in the Middle East until humanity becomes capable of seeing a wider picture than preferring war to pretty much anything else but it might shift the human race one step further towards it. And if that's all that can be done right now, it still has to be done. Not Dr Barker because she has done her job and she's not an archaeologist. This is *my* job. And I've been told it is yours, too.

'May I ask by whom?'

'By God of course,' he said. 'Who else?'

I began to giggle; I couldn't help it.

'I'm not laughing at you,' I managed to get out before the giggle grew into a guffaw. 'It's just the whole ridiculous situation!'

'I take it this is not precisely the kind of conversation you expect to be having with a stranger from another century on first acquaintance?' said Ben, poker-faced.

That was it; the giggle erupted and I simply couldn't stop laughing. Fortunately it was infectious laughter and in less than a minute we were both choking and gasping so much that we had to lean against a couple of tree trunks to stay vertical.

'Enough already!' said Ben, mopping his eyes with a brightly-coloured handkerchief. He sat down on an only-vaguely-wet grass bank and I joined him. A blackbird, spooked, cried 'pink-pink-pink' and flew away.

'It's a big project,' he said. 'But amazingly I have funding. Not a huge amount but it's reputable and I have permission to hire you as an expert, given your authorship of *Mother of God*. The idea was to scout out possible locations for the First Temple around the Kidron and dig where we can.

'The big question right now is can you get leave of absence for a few months? It's likely to take all of that. And I'd like to start by the beginning of next month.'

'Oh I don't think that will be the slightest problem,' I replied with a smile. 'Now, please tell me about this strange and, frankly, ridiculous marriage of yours. Maisie was at least forty years older than you and you barely even seem to have met. What on Earth is that about?'

'It's private,' he said. And that, even more ridiculously, was that.

Chapter Ten

I BOOKED MY flight to Tel Aviv for a fortnight later.

Probably most of us have an old childhood memory of being told that we were going on holiday in two weeks' time and I remember being so very excited and wondering how I could bear the eternity of waiting a whole fourteen days before we left.

For grown-ups, it's more like 'How the hell am I going to get everything done in just two weeks?'

In my case, there was a Dean to deal with as well as what to do with my home. And an assistant vicar who might well still be vulnerable to possession despite half a dozen bee stings and a distinct wetting with holy elderflower champagne (I've no idea why bee stings seem to expel demons but maybe it's the shock?). There was also the vague but real threat to my witchy friend who didn't exactly endear herself to the parish council for chucking the flower cocktail at the assistant vicar, not to mention telling her inaccurately that she was quite safe from the bees; and of course, admin, admin, sodding admin. I was totally overwhelmed with admin despite Mrs Tiggy's acerbic help.

And there was Jon… who was moving on, too, and keen to have me help him tie up what he called 'loose ends' in the afterlife. Within a very short time to come, there would be no more nightly trips together. You don't stay static in the heavens. That old 'and like stars, his children crowned, all in white, shall wait around' stuff from *Once In Royal David's City* which made the teenage me go 'how *boring!*' simply isn't the case. It's all growth and moving on. 'Further up and further in' as Farsight the eagle calls out at the end of C. S. Lewis's *The Last Battle*.

That would have been such a huge loss had my life not changed trajectory, too. Apparently it is possible to continue the work with another companion but that wasn't the plan for me.

However, there was still grieving to do. Yes, I know life goes on after death (who better?); yes I know there's still plenty of life ahead of me here; yes I know that it's all in the Divine Plan; yes I know I don't have any relatives (or even many friends) I'll leave behind; yes I know I'll be able to see and be with Jon—and my parents and other wonderful souls—when I die, but I like it here on Earth.

But there's absolutely no point whatsoever in going on whinging to a dead person that you don't want to die. There will be no sympathy, just a blank look that says 'and your point is?'

'Cheer up,' said Jon. 'It might never happen.'

'Of course it's going to happen!' I said. 'Everybody dies!'

'Yes, but unless your death is set in stone because of some extraordinary destiny (which yours, by the way, is not), the dream is still only a probability. You might last another fifty years.

'You think so?'

'No, I don't. But you might.'

'Oh thanks a bunch.'

'You're welcome,' said my annoying big brother, steering around a rather large, flaming asteroid.

What carried me through those days was a deep sense of gratitude that somehow this must all be meant. That the problems and suspension were needed to ensure I was free for this great (and unsettling) adventure. What would happen if we could find the ancient First Temple? What if there were still some artefacts hidden that we could find? The Hebrew writings are confused on what went missing between the fall of the First Temple and the building of the Second. Some of the lost items may have been taken away for safe keeping, by those devoted to the temple tradition. Others would have been destroyed. And what of the Menorah? Just one would be worth a king's ransom. Ten or even eleven? That's an awful lot of gold.

That First Temple honoured both sacred masculine and divine feminine with wine and bread and incense. The goddess had been evicted from the temple by King Josiah and that destruction probably included the items removed in the purge or remembered as missing from the Second Temple. Items named the Asherah, the host of heaven, the horses for the sun, *a* Menorah (not all the Menorot), the anointing oil, the manna, the high priest's staff that bore almond blossoms, the ark, the fire and the Spirit. A long list and, for us, a confusing one but all there in Biblical writings. Some sources say that what I'm assuming is the 'great' menorah, behind the veil that I saw in my visit, vanished forever but as one is shown in architecture being taken into Rome following the sack of the second temple in 70 CE it's all incredibly unclear. The topic of the actual number of candlesticks that had been in either the First or the Second Temple would probably keep a Yeshivah of Rabbis debating for about a decade. A British vicar's vision would not exactly be taken seriously.

In the Book of Revelation John writes of the ark restored to the Holy of Holies, (Rev.11.19) and we all know about the four horses that ride out from the temple including the 'pale horse' of death (Rev. 6.1-8). He saw a Man in the midst of a lighted menorah (Rev.1.12) and he heard the Spirit promising the faithful that they would recover the hidden manna (Rev.2.17). It does rather look as though John was describing the restoration of the First Temple. He also saw the Queen of Heaven in the temple, even though she is not named as Queen. 'A great sign appeared in heaven, a woman clothed with the sun, with the moon under her feet and on her head a crown of twelve stars' (Rev.12.1). Ironically—or maybe not?—you can see her in many a statue of the Virgin Mary throughout Mediterranean Europe. At her feet in the Book of Revelation lay a great red dragon. She gave birth to a son who was destined to fulfil Psalm number two in ruling the nations with a rod of iron. Personally I prefer to translate it as 'a staff of stars', given that archaeology believes that iron was discovered by the Hittites of ancient Egypt somewhere around the time of the First Temple. They found and extracted it from meteorites and used the ore to make spearheads, tools and trinkets.

However, in the midst of all this magic, as Ben also pointed out, was the worrying possibility of animal sacrifice starting up again should we find the original temple and it were to be restored. The First Temple, remember, had sacrifices of bread and wine, just like Christianity. Yes, there *were* animal sacrifices but it wasn't obligatory and certainly the temple wasn't the charnel house it had become by Jesus's time.

How do we know that? Because of the Elephantine papyri discovered at the beginning of the twentieth century. Elephantine is an island on the River Nile that had a 'House of Yahweh' serving a Hebrew military garrison and refugees from the Babylonian invasion. This temple was destroyed by the Egyptians because the cult of Khnum objected to blood sacrifices there; Khnum, being a ram-headed god, took it rather personally. When permission came from the Egyptian governor to rebuild the temple there only meal offerings and incense were to be allowed (Pap.32) Another papyrus states that no sheep, bulls or goats were to be sacrificed there, only meal, incense and drink offerings (Pap 33). There had been a previous temple there for more than a century with apparently no objections to its practices which, historians believe, is strong evidence for no animal sacrifices to the Holy One before the Second Temple in Jerusalem. In fact, there's some pretty convincing evidence that the Second Temple was funded by the Persian King, Darius, *on condition* that it had animal sacrifice.

Corruption is not new...

But I suspect I am boring you now. It's just that all this history was being refreshed in my mind before heading off to discover if we could discover Solomon's temple—and Bathsheba's grave.

Maisie's funeral went pretty well, even though Mrs Tiggy and a few others were only there to make sure the old harridan was safely dead and buried. Ben—still in his nineteenth century clothing, this time including a cravat—gave a short and revealing eulogy about a difficult start in life in being raised by a widowed father who cared more for horses and hounds than for the daughter whose birth had killed his wife, and about her gruff kindness to Ben himself. He forbore to mention that she thought her remaining family were a total waste of space but the essence of it was still there, nestling between the lines. He didn't mention any weird kind of marriage.

The wake was better attended than the funeral, mostly because the drinks were free and Judy at the King's Arms makes the best pasties outside of Cornwall. Ben and I had half an hour's discussion as originally planned afterwards, before he headed back to the Middle East.

'You are coming, aren't you?' he said as he shook my hand in leaving. 'I want to get to know you a lot better.' He had catapulted into my life just after the moon was full and I was beginning to wonder if this strange hook-nosed man was, indeed, my anam cara.

And then there was the Dean. He had, apparently, managed to introduce himself to Alessina, the bee-sting swollen Lucie and the parish council and then headed off home, only to get his assistant to phone the next day 'to arrange a lunch before you leave.' It had to be done and I did want to go shopping in Exbridge for something suitable to wear on my feet in the Holy Land. And that was pretty much a whole blessed day away from the admin.

I was expecting to walk together from the cathedral offices to a restaurant but instead we had a picnic in Northernhay Gardens. Xander met me at the door, handed me a folded rug and guided me away from any listening ears. He was carrying an old-fashioned basket with a red gingham cover and the neck of a bottle of San Pellegrino and another of white wine sticking out.

We walked while exchanging trivia about the weather and the rebuilding of the Royal Clarendon Hotel which had burned down nearly a decade earlier. I saw no sign of Margot, his ghost white German Shepherd, nor of his guardian.

'Who made this?' I asked as we sat down on the rug with our backs to the war memorial. Xander was laying out china plates and Tupperware filled with cheese, sourdough bread rolls, processed meats, olives and hard-boiled eggs. Cutlery was wrapped in cloth napkins; there was salt and pepper and a little pot of butter.

'Sophie, my wife,' he said and I thought he was blushing slightly. Understandable, given that he'd kissed me in St. Raphael's. I wondered what Sophie thought of preparing a picnic for a strange female vicar from the sticks but, probably wisely, I said no more. We had enough to unravel without that.

We served ourselves in silence and began to eat.

'I'm sorry,' said Xander, just too soon before swallowing a piece of bread and cheese. The resulting choking and coughing ended up with my banging his back until he recovered and did quite a lot to dissolve the tension.

'Shall I start?' I said, realising that Xander wasn't exactly loquacious.

'Please.' He waved his napkin at me spreading, crumbs everywhere. 'Oh bugger.'

'It's okay. Just relax,' I said. 'I don't bite. Let's see if I can sum things up.

'Right… you and I are part of a team of living humans, world-wide, who have had death experiences and therefore are able to travel between life and death as long as we are accompanied by a discarnate soul who is engaged in soul-retrieval.

'It's my understanding that they need us because we still live in the coarser aspects of the psyche so we can connect better with the dead who don't realise that they *have* a soul and don't know how to go through to the other worlds.

'We're picked up by someone—in my case it's my dead brother—each night and deposited back about five minutes later having lived probably half a day elsewhere.

'It's got to be exhausting as we are living double lives in ridiculous timeframes. It's easier for me because I don't have family; I have no idea how you cope being married—'

I stopped as Xander put his head in his hands. 'Oh God, yes,' he said. 'It's a nightmare.'

'So, I guess it might help us both to talk about it?' I said. 'That'll be why you took us away from listening ears in the offices.

'Oh—and I had a ghost dog for a while too. She was a hound. She's gone back through now because I helped her reunite with her forever-owner and I miss her. I know about Margot because I was shown the time when you found her spirit with her puppies in Ukraine and I've seen you now and then on the other side but not often. I saw Margot when we met in your office but I don't know where she is now.'

'She comes and goes,' said Xander. 'I suppose, like your ghost dog, she is here for a reason but her forever home is in the heavens. I love her but to be honest she is a complicated added… um… complication. Sorry, I ran out of words there.'

I told him that I got the emphasis and we spent a while trading stories of the afterlife. It seemed that his spiritual other half was otherwise a stranger and he had none of the cosy travel and chat which I had with Jon. He had 'died' in a skiing accident which meant he was still in some pain and having physiotherapy for damage to his back apart, from losing one foot. 'To be honest, the Work is almost a relief because nothing hurts on the other side and I have two fully-working legs,' he said.

We talked about Rus-El and my going invisible and how he'd felt totally abandoned when I left the church without him and he had to create some kind of story (poor sweet baby—not) but that Alessina had been all that was kind apart from the sticky drink-throwing incident and had seemed to understand what had been going on.

'She's my best friend,' I said. I didn't add, 'and a witch.'

I guess we made our peace over that picnic. I told him the truth of everything concerning the Bishop and Xander confirmed that he had carried out an exorcism on him—at Xavier's request—and there had been no re-infiltration. It was all going quite well and the food was good. I refused wine, tempting though it was. Xander drank two glasses.

'The bishop is hideously embarrassed about it all,' he said. Well, you would be wouldn't you? 'He'd really like to see you again and make amends.'

Oh he would, would he? And yet here I am, suspended. I was about to say something somewhat emphatic to that effect when Hero floated words across my mind. They sounded like 'snap-shut!' and I felt her figurative wings wrap around me, pulling in my energy field; the one that had been relaxing quite peacefully and looking forward to what might or might not be a home-made French lemon tartlet.

'Oh! Isn't that him? What a coincidence!' said Xander failing totally to sound in any way coincidental. 'What a coincidence!' he repeated.

Coincidence my arse. Dammit, this was nothing but a set up.

No, that wasn't quite fair; Xander and I had needed to talk but even so… now, apart from anything else, I was surrounded by men with names beginning with X. The sooner both of them were exes in my life the better, came the unbidden but totally understandable thought.

'Oh goodness me!' I said for the sake of delicacy as 'What the actual *fuck?*' probably wouldn't be helpful. 'Well, what a good thing you packed an extra lemon tart.' Xander got the full-on over-egged irony and had the grace to look embarrassed.

'Ah! Xander! Amabel! What a pleasant surprise!' said the Bishop, wandering casually over from behind a convenient row of trees. 'May I join you?'

'Er…' said Xander.

'Fuck off,' said my electro-magnetic field. 'Of course,' said my mouth which was trying very hard not to bare its teeth.

Hold, whispered Hero. I'm never quite sure whether she means 'I'm holding you' or 'hold back.' Probably both.

Reveal, she said. And as Xavier sat down cross-legged on the edge of the tartan rug, I saw his guardian and Xander's guardian, too. And I knew exactly why Margot was no longer there…

'Oh good grief,' I said. And without anyone's approval, I got up and ran.

Chapter Eleven

THEY DIDN'T SEE me go, of course. They didn't see me at all from that moment. At least the humans didn't. At least *that* 'good grief!' was intentional.

Interesting fact: guardian angels can be possessed as well. Who'd have thought?

Rus-El! I screamed inside my head, diving behind a useful ice-cream van and trying to decide where to go, while my feet seemed to be going in all directions. Was it safe to get back to the car? Stuff the shopping. They probably have clothes for sale in Israel.

'His eyes were fine! Alessina exorcised him!' I hissed at Hero. Also 'FFS, am I clear?!'

We are both clear, said Hero. She refrained from saying *It's not all about you.*

'How?'

Stroppy girls easier to clear.

Really? Angels know the word 'stroppy'? Okay. That's one for the feminists, I guess.

'But you would say that!' I was now scooting round the cathedral heading for the car.

Hero appeared to me in all her beauty on the other side of my little Renault. Understood. Trust*!*

'I'm changing my ticket and heading for the airport,' I said.

No. Alessina.

'Okay.' And as Hero said 'Alessina,' I felt fear descend.

'Has something happened?'

?

Stupid question. Somethings are always happening. There's rarely a moment when something doesn't happen.

'Is she in danger?'

Yes.

I saw the pall of smoke almost as soon as I left Exbridge. There's a speed camera on the A30 from Exbridge to Okehampton and quite rightly, too. I'll deal with the consequences another day. It was unmistakably a house or barn fire and I found my jaw and shoulders clenched as I shot off the A30 and wound my way through the lanes. I was, briefly, stuck behind one of the ever-present tractors but luckily all the local farmers know my car and, if I come up behind them at speed, they are generally far more biddable to pulling into the nearest lay-by than they would be for your average tourist. I blew a kiss to the farmer and negotiated my way as courteously as possible past a dog walker and three cyclists.

Two miles to go and I heard the fire engines' bells; one mile to go and I saw the ambulance. It was Luke and Alessina's house they were heading for and God knows how two fire engines actually got up that steep and narrow lane to the hollow where that lovely witch's cottage lay.

Paramedics were racing up the drive on foot as I pulled in behind the ambulance (and yes I did leave enough space for them) and I, too, ran up that hill, smoke making me cough.

The thatch was ablaze. Alessina's car was there. The neighbours were briefing one of the firemen and both the paramedics and there was someone lying on the grass of the front garden. Luke, by the look of it.

'Alessina?' I shouted both to my friend and the neighbours.

'Still in there, we think,' said a tall, balding man. 'The hall's ablaze. Can't get in.'

'Round the back!' I said and dived off. A fireman tried to stop me but I wasn't having any. I knew where Alessina's treatment room was and it had its own entrance. At the side of the cottage there is a largish pond and without even an apology to the wildlife, I jumped right into it to make myself as wet as possible and pulled my shirt up to cover my mouth and nose before ramming my shoulder up against the back door. It was the right decision; touching the handle would have burnt my hands. The door gave and I was inside, holding my breath and diving into Alessina's room at the back.

She was there, face down, spreadeagled on the floor. A fire

in the grate but no actual flames in the room and she was not obviously burnt. Smoke inhalation? I only had time to turn her over before three burly firemen burst into the room behind me.

'*Idiot!*' one spat at me and pushed me back outside while the other two lifted Alessina and carried her to safety.

I'm pretty sure they attempted to read me the riot act outside but I wasn't listening; I may even have told them to fuck off as I tried to focus on what the paramedics were doing. They do a wonderful job, by the way; no doubt about that but I was stark staring, bat-shit crazy by then.

'Blow to the side of the head,' said one paramedic. They began CPR right there on the grass as the house continued to burn. I fell on my knees, soaking wet and redolent with tears and began to pray as I've never prayed before.

They wouldn't take me in the ambulance because (a) I was soaking wet and (b) there really wasn't room with Luke also unconscious (though apparently not in any danger). So I waited and watched and prayed with the neighbours as the fire brigade put out the fire and when Raymond and Ruth arrived home we were able to offer some small amount of comfort and support. Police were there by then, too—the firemen said it was clearly arson—I earwigged them telling the first two police officers that there appeared to be the remains of a can that had contained petrol just inside the unlocked front door and that's where the fire had started. I managed to invoke Inspector Eleanor Marks's name and was able to weigh in by adding that Alessina had a head wound which wasn't explained by smoke inhalation. The still-smoking house was blocked off by blue-and-white tape. I didn't mention any rogue villagers but I knew that word had gone around that Norris had a problem with the local witch.

The neighbours, Paula and Simon, drove Raymond and Ruth straight to Exbridge to the hospital and promised to put them up for the night, too. The house wasn't all that badly damaged — it was certainly repairable but it wasn't going to be habitable for quite a while.

We agreed a phone trail for updates (and understandably, I was close to the end of that trail) and with a cold and suspicious heart

I drove away, parked outside my house and strode off to the other side of the village to visit Norris Whipple.

He was home, watering the garden, a picture of innocence and, interestingly, seemingly not at all interested in what would be the talk of the village for weeks—the pall of smoke still hanging in the air to the west.

'Ah, Mr Whipple,' I said, brightly. 'I've run out of petrol. I don't suppose you'd happen to have a spare can?'

'No!' he said, far too swiftly. 'I don't have a can of petrol.'

'Oh? I was sure you did have one,' I lied, breezily. 'Colin said you always had one in the shed for emergencies, given that we're miles from a petrol station.'

'I got rid of it,' he said. 'It wasn't needed.'

'When did you get rid of it?'

'What's it to you?'

'Nothing to me,' I said. 'Possibly everything to the people whose house just caught fire at the other end of the village. Someone might have stolen your petrol can to do the job.'

'Oh,' he said, uncertainly.

We stood with eyes locked for a few moments. Norris's eyes were those of someone who lived life on automatic prejudices without waking up to reality at all but they didn't seem demonic. But I'm not being terribly good at spotting that kind of thing at the moment.

'Well, never mind,' I said. 'I'm sure someone else can help me with some petrol. Did you see which house it was that was attacked?'

'Um. No,' he said. 'Whose?'

'You didn't go and look or ask?' I said. 'How strange. It was Alessina's and Luke's house.' They are both in hospital. So I suppose your wish has been granted. Somebody *did* do something about that woman you accused of being a witch.

'Mr Whipple, obviously as a Christian, you will be praying for their swift recovery, yes?'

He mumbled something and turned away but I wasn't having that.

'Yes, Mr Whipple? You'll be praying for healing?'

'No,' he said. 'She deserves all she got. I had nothing to do with it—and don't you dare try and accuse me—but she deserves all she got.'

'Father forgive him; he doesn't know what he is doing,' I said, clearly and walked away.

I began to cry as I headed back home. I had no idea whether Alessina lived or died and I didn't know how to find out; she'd barely be at the hospital yet and no one needed me to be nagging the family for answers. I would have to wait.

Died, then lived, like you said Hero, gently. Trust.

There are definitely some advantages to being bonkers; I felt comforted.

At home, I called Mrs Tiggy and left a message for Lucie asking them both to come over. Lucie replied with a classic text: 'Before or after Evening snog?' which I assumed meant 'Evensong.' Usually I'd laugh out loud but today was being a bit of a week… Much as I wanted to stay in the village and be with my friend (assuming she *did* live) my going would be the best gift I could give her and her family—for now, at least. They could all stay here while I was away to give them time to sort out the damage to the house.

While I waited for my assistant and my fiery PA-cum-housekeeper I wrote out my will. It's easy enough to do if you know the wording and I'd done it many times but this time was different; this time was in case I didn't come back from Israel. Lucie and Mrs Tiggy could witness it and I could also make it clear to them both that the house was for Luke, Alessina and the children in the meantime.

You get sneaky when you are dealing with the un-manifest and I hadn't told anyone that I was heading for Israel. Ben had been working in Iraq and he didn't want the project out in the open so hopefully he would have kept schtum as well. Instead I'd been rather vague about possibly doing yoga in Bali or going to an Ashram. No one who knew me really well would have been fooled by either—but at least I wasn't laying out obvious tracks.

Then I booked a flight to New York and a bus to Heathrow and a taxi to Exbridge, I printed off my telephone contacts list and, by the time Lucie and Mrs Tiggy arrived, I was packed.

I told them I was now leaving tomorrow and both women were initially shocked that I was going away with my best friend's life in the balance and violence in the village. I couldn't really explain that I was fleeing both Dean and Bishop. Lucie had arrived with her boyfriend Will—the formerly homeless man who had saved my life once in the cathedral. He was now a born-again Christian planning to train for ministry and had long forgotten that he had ever had a crush on me. But I'd had a weird demonic-parallel universe experience with him when he had believed that I was his for the taking and I wouldn't trust him as far as I could throw him. She'd, understandably, probably brought him to ensure she wouldn't be saying Evensong to a completely empty church but he was rather surplus to requirements.

'Alessina needs our prayers, not our physical presence,' I scolded back when Will tried to shame me into staying in the village.

'I thought she was your friend!' both he and Lucie had said repeatedly. 'How can you leave at a time like this?'

Mrs Tiggy, bless her, got it. 'She's leaving them the house to stay in,' she said, nodding her head. 'Very kind and very sensible. They'll not want to be involved in parish affairs so best it all moves to your official house right now, Lucie. After all, this house is Bel's in its entirety, not belonging to the church.'

She turned to me. 'I'll keep the house fresh for them and look after them,' she said. I can do that while diverting calls to Lucie while you're away.'

'Bless you,' I said, gratefully and, after the will was duly signed (no they didn't see what it said), put in a sealed envelope and given to Mrs Tiggy, I chased them all away.

'Take this,' I said to Mrs Tiggy, giving her my mobile phone as Lucie and Will walked off towards the church hand in hand.

'Why?' she said.

'Because you'll need to stay up to date with Alessina and that's the phone the calls will come in on,' I said. 'I'm going off-grid for a while.'

'Hmm. More of that sorcery stuff?' said Mrs Tiggy, who knew perfectly well what she meant.

'I'm afraid so. Don't trust the Bishop and don't trust the Dean.

And while you're at it, don't trust Will,' I said. 'Sorry, but it's for the best.'

'Will I see you before you go?' said Mrs Tiggy.

'No.'

'Hmph. Let me know how you get on. On this phone, right?'

'Yes, I will.'

She nodded at me; Mrs Tiggy didn't do hugs. I watched her bustle away and sighed.

Margot emerged from the hallway behind me and, idly, I stroked her invisible ears. I could *just* feel her presence and I could definitely see her shadowy form.

'I can't help him,' I said. 'I have to do my own work.'

But I knew I could try so, in the hour before the taxi arrived, I said a special Mass of Deliverance for both the Bishop and the Dean (and their guardian angels). I made up a lot of the liturgy with guidance from Ariel and Hero and, at their insistence, I invoked a form of Rus-El for both men to protect them and their angels in future. I didn't know if it would work as well as I hoped but Margot thumped her tail at me and pushed her nose into my hand in thanks.

'Are you coming with me?' I asked. It seemed so and even if she were a ghost, I would be glad of the company.

Two hours later I walked into the Royal Devon and Exbridge Hospital in my dog collar and shamelessly used my profession to get my own way. Vicars are allowed places where no one else but close family can go. I was guided to the ward where Alessina lay, unconscious and with a bandaged head but alive. She was on oxygen and her life signs were good. Luke was in a separate ward and awake. Both the children had gone back to the village with the neighbours.

I sat with Luke for a few minutes, telling him that my house was his for the duration and that he wasn't to worry about the bills or anything; they were all on standing order. I gave him my keys, reassured him that Alessina was going to be okay although she did have quite a serious head wound so would have to stay in hospital for a while and asked him to give her my love.

Then I took the night bus to Heathrow and flew to New York.

Chapter Twelve

I DON'T LIKE cities much and New York is a pretty crazy city but it's a good place to be anonymous and you can amuse yourself annoying people in the street by beaming at them and saying 'hello!' as you walk past. I had come here on impulse, simply because it was nowhere that anyone who knew me would expect me to go. I wanted to lie low for a while and, ironically, to rest in the city that never sleeps.

Only Jon knew I was here and, apart from checking in occasionally, he left me in peace. We'd only been travelling together for about a year but the stopping of the nightly trips was pretty unsettling. I missed him already but I knew he had to move on. And if my dream was correct, I wouldn't be that far behind.

I wasn't lonely because I had Margot. I'm not sure *why* I had Margot but one of the advantages of a ghost dog, apart from a comforting kind of weight next to you on the bed at night, was that her presence meant that Marcus could visit me.

I had bought a couple of burner phones so I could find out how Alessina was doing but, in fact, Marcus was the one who updated me with news. He said it was a good excuse to visit and I found that it was a strange and rather lovely feeling to be tourist guide to a ghost. I'd fallen for Marcus in a big way when Jon introduced us; he's a dog wrangler on the other side, guiding our beloved pets through and helping them meld back into their soul groups so they don't grieve for their human pets. I suspect he's one of thousands of Marcuses (is that a word?) but this one was *my* Marcus. Margot stayed with us and the three of us spent a couple of hours a day wandering the streets together with Marcus's nineteenth-century consciousness both amusing and amazing me in his reactions to our crazy modern world. When I asked him how he had the time to be with me, he said time was incredibly fluid and not to worry about it, so I didn't.

I was wary of him at first because I'd been fooled before by a Marcus-like apparition—which turned out to be Will—which ended in a kind of date-rape but, as day spread into day and all I experienced was good company, I relaxed. I'm sure you want to know if and how a human and a ghost can make love but all I'll say is to suggest a look at the 1960s movie *Barbarella*. It's not like that but it's somewhere in the ballpark.

For those two weeks I was amazingly happy.

It helped to know that Alessina was doing well. She had a fractured skull but was awake, sentient and recovering. Luke and the children had moved into my house (browbeaten into accepting the offer by a fearsome Mrs Tiggy) and Norris Whipple had been questioned by the police. No charges, as of yet at least, but investigations were ongoing. Petrol had been identified as the starting-point of the fire and there were fingerprints on the stone which had been thrown through the window and which hit Alessina.

Thanking God I was on paid leave, I bought myself some suitable clothing for digging in the Middle East and, when the time had come, flew back to Heathrow in time to change flights and head out to Tel Aviv. Marcus went back to the heavens (but with gentle intention to meet again if we could) and Margot went with him. Part of me wondered if I should tell the Dean but good sense told me to keep firmly out of contact.

I'd kept in touch with Ben Fairfax via one of the burner phones and he sent a car to Ben Gurion airport to meet me. From there it was less than an hour to the site he believed would turn out to be the location of the Hebrew First Temple. It was just above the Valley of Jehoshaphat, alternatively called The Valley of Decision, featured in the Book of Joel: '*I will gather all the nations and bring them down to the valley of Jehoshaphat, and I will enter into judgment with them there, on account of my people and my heritage Israel, because they have scattered them among the nations.*' Fortunately for us, that part of the Nahal Qidron area was pretty much uninhabited.

His theory worked mainly on archaeological theory that the First Temple had running water. I couldn't exactly say, 'yes, I've seen it' but where the dig was located was on the side of one of the crinkly hills, suggesting that the temple itself had been built into the land, a little like the fabled rock buildings of Petra. Those are now supposed to be part of a royal tomb and given that tradition says a Kohen, or priestly descendant, cannot cross a graveyard, it was one controversial aspect of the dig. If it was a grave as well as the temple there would be all sorts of shenanigans about it.

Like so much of Jewish law, this is debatable to some extent. Some say the Levitical text refers to enclosed spaces or unburied bodies; others that any kind of burial ground itself is a no-no. Orthodox cemeteries generally have a separate burial ground for Kohanim and their families which is at a distance from the everyday people's cemetery, so that the relatives of Kohanim can be visited by a Kohen without their having to enter the graveyard. There's a huge Muslim graveyard in front of the sealed-up Golden Gate of Jerusalem through which Christ is supposed to enter the city at the Second Coming. It was built simply to prevent him from doing so, given that he's presumed to be a Kohen, though I suspect, should that event ever happen, it really wouldn't be a problem for the Son of God. Anyway, aren't they all supposed to resurrect physically when he comes?

It's also moot as to whether gentile dead bodies have the same effect on the priestly class. As I was, secretly, looking for Bathsheba's grave, I was hoping against hope that temple and grave were either separate or somehow compatible.

'Tell me again why you need me here,' I said to Ben over supper the first night. We were having falafel and stuffed vine leaves from a street kitchen on the outskirts of Jerusalem and trying hard not to feel depressed at the still-obvious fall-out and wreckage from the recent Middle Eastern war. I'd already met Ali who was our Field Director, managing the small group of field technicians who did the majority of the excavating. She was a small, dark-skinned woman in her mid-twenties who wore a hijab and kept both arms and legs covered despite the sun. Ali had a PhD in the Abyssinian origins of the Tree of Life legend and was a busy, quicksilver kind of person, always tapping a finger or swinging a foot even when resting. She overflowed with the vibrant energy of youth and enthusiasm, making me feel very old and rather out-at-elbow, but she was friendly and welcoming.

Ben was our Principal Investigator, in charge of the whole shebang. 'You're our specialist,' he said. 'Neither of us is published in the mainstream. You've done the major research on the First Temple and you'll be our spokesperson as to why it *is* the First Temple for when we find it.'

'Oh great,' I said, unenthusiastically, secretly beginning to plot exactly why I wouldn't be pushing myself in front of any TV cameras if push came to shove. Fortunately I could see that Ben was naturally a showman and I suspected he would enjoy the limelight. His working clothes were still pretty antiquated with a spotted cravat adorning his open-necked shirt and a natty linen waistcoat in cream. His magnificent nose poked out beyond his battered Panama and seemed to spend most of its time peeling from the sun.

Archaeological digs are a lot more boring than TV makes them seem. Yes, there are amazing discoveries but mostly it's incredibly careful digging, a lot of dashed hopes and a fair amount of pottery from any time over the last thousand years. There were seven of us in all, some with more faith than others as to whether we'd succeed, and Ben was strangely tight-lipped about how he'd worked out this possible location. Oh, he'd say it was because of the running water and gesture towards me but there had to be more to it than that.

I asked him if it were intuition or guidance. After all, if he could see the ghostly me he could surely have at least one foot in the field of mystics.

'I suppose so,' he said. 'If a Jewish atheist can possibly be a mystic.'

'You do know, don't you, that the Romans called Jews, 'licensed atheists' because if their God couldn't be seen or described, they considered Him not to be any God at all.' I said. 'And at the risk of sounding trite, I'll line myself up with the Lubavitch Rabbi Sholom Dovber who said he didn't believe in the God the atheists don't believe in, either.'

'Yes, that is trite. Don't hesitate to voice any other unasked-for information, anytime,' said Ben, squashingly, tearing off a corner of flatbread and dipping it in peppery olive oil. Squashingly is a genuine word, by the way; I looked it up.

Actually, I laughed. He was quite right. 'Nerves,' I said. 'But I will certainly offer unasked-for information if it's relevant to the dig.'

'Good,' he said, drinking peppermint tea. 'Why are you nervous?'

'I haven't been on a dig for decades and with a lot of missing memory I might not be as useful as you hoped. I'm worried about your relying on my expertise on its own.'

'Ah, but to paraphrase the admirable Russel Crowe in *Noah*, your expertise is not on its own, is it?' said Ben. '*You* are closer to the horse's mouth.'

'I am? But you don't believe in the horse's mouth!'

'Yes, you are,' he said, patting his lips with a paper napkin and getting up from the table. 'And just because I don't believe in something doesn't mean it doesn't exist.'

Abruptly, he added: 'I'm going to see a man about a parchment. I'll see you all tomorrow,' and headed off towards the expedition's Land Rover.

But we didn't see him the following morning. When Ali and I rolled out of our beds—we shared a cheap Airbnb with one bedroom and two single beds—Ben was nowhere to be seen. After a moment's panic, we checked our phones to find a message to say he had gone to Kiriath Jearim to talk to someone about the Ark of the Covenant and would be back by evening.

'And that is Ben,' said Ali, in her soft, Palestinian-accented voice. 'He will go to every source of information no matter how trivial. To my annoyance, it is a system which often works. He discovers more through people's memories than in digging our holes, even though the memories cannot possibly remember that distance.'

We were sharing a Middle Eastern breakfast of pickled meats and vegetables with bread and figs. This was definitely a self-catering trip and I was glad to know there was a 'dig car' that we could all use. I would be able to contribute once I could get to some shops. We spent the morning on what had already been discovered. Ali, all busy-ness, showed me the permits, the land which had already been cleared and marked out, what had been found so far—the usual pottery from the Middle Ages from my first, cursory glance—and introduced me to our field workers, Mo, David, Jakob, Asher, Delyth, Isa and Malin. Delyth, being a red-headed Welsh giantess, literally stood out like a sore thumb with her red, sunburnt skin. She was slathering on sun cream to the taunts of 'too late, dumbass!' from Asher and Isa and had a wry smile that acknowledged her error with attractive good humour.

I felt incredibly at home. Apart from the glorious ridiculousness of our leader going to talk to someone about the Ark of the Covenant as though it was sitting in their living room for him to collect, this world of archaeology had been my home for at least two decades. Although I couldn't recall much in my brain, my hands and feet remembered everything and I found myself working on the dig with the others entirely naturally and sharing in their banter. My body luxuriated in the Middle Eastern sun.

Everyone spoke English, although the others dipped in and out of their respective languages with each other. My Arabic was poor but I could pick up most of what Jakob and Asher said to each other and, of course, Delyth's voice had that softly powerful Welsh magic to it. As is usually the case, those whose language was familiar tended to stick together so it was Delyth and I; Ali, Malin and Mo; Jakob, David, Asher and Isa, in three teams, calling out to each other in the common language but holding to their own for general conversation.

By lunchtime, I realised that I was happier than I had been for years and that was a bit of a shock. After all, ministry is meant to put you into the sublime world of the Divine—and sometimes it does—but the joy of this included having no responsibilities for other people's problems, beliefs or dramas; we were just looking for something and cherishing what we found.

It was Delyth who had found the site where we were currently digging. She was what's called a 'geomancer' which made me boggle until I remembered that my best friend was a witch. Every day, she wandered up and down and around the site with two copper dowsing rods in her hands, asking questions of the spirits and the stones. You could scoff all you liked but when Delyth stopped and said, 'dig here, there's a wall two feet down,' and you dug two feet down, you'd find the remains of a wall.

'Why doesn't every archaeological site have a dowser?' I asked after one day of watching and attending to Hero, who was talking with Delyth's guardian.

'Because it's nothing but wanky bollocks,' said Delyth cheerfully, sitting down and unwrapping a half-melted bar of chocolate. 'Want some?'

'Wanky bollocks? I think I've got enough of my own,' I said, holding my hand out for a soft piece of dark brown heaven.

'How do you ask if it is the temple?' I said.

'You tune in and say, "Show me Soloman's Temple,' she replied, easily. 'It's not rocket science.'

'So have you walked all over these hills?'

'Nope. I stood near the Temple Mount and asked which direction to go to find the First Temple,' she said. 'Try them yourself. Anyone can do it if they want to.'

'What do I ask?' I said, holding the rods and noting that the handles had loose copper sheaths so I couldn't physically control how they moved.

'Whatever you like. "Show me underground water; show me an underground wall; show me the Holy of Holies,' said Delyth.

Ask permission whispered Hero.

Of whom? I thought.

Spirit of the Land. And protection. Wild work.

I liked the thought of 'wild work' and then, after a moment, I wasn't so sure. I knew there were nature spirits and I knew they were amoral (not *im*moral, *a*moral, which means they have no concept of any kind of morals so couldn't adopt one if they wanted to. Think *Midsummer Night's Dream*).

'Do you ask permission?' I said.

Delyth looked at me sideways. 'Hmm,' she said. 'You know your stuff, don't you? Not bad for a vicar.'

'Who told you I was a vicar?' I said, slightly peevishly.

'Ben, of course,' she said. 'But he said you weren't at all the preachy kind.'

'I hope not!'

I took the rods and closed my eyes. *Mother of this land*, I thought. *May I have your permission to search for Bathsheba's grave?*

Protection, said Hero again.

Rus-El!

Good.

Sensing the red angel beside me, I asked again. And got a distinct feeling of a breeze in my hair and a soft 'yes, child, you may.'

'Show me Bathsheba's grave,' I said out loud.

'What?' said Delyth.

Both dowsing rods slowly turned to my right.

'Oh my God,' she said, jumping up. 'Follow them!'

So we did.

Chapter Thirteen

'So, WHY ARE you looking for Bathsheba's grave?' asked Delyth as we walked carefully over the dry, rocky ground in the direction that the dowsing rods showed. 'Do you think it could be connected with the temple?'

'I had a dream,' I said cautiously. 'Actually I had a couple of dreams.'

'Ah!' There was no other response and we kept walking. All of us were walking (although angels don't, technically, walk). I could sense Ariel, Rus-El and also Delyth's guardian beside us and I felt a powerful, yet soft, sense of excitement tinged with that old enemy of all of us, a 'healthy' doubt.

'Can it actually be this easy?' I said.

'No,' said Delyth, stopping and shading her eyes with her right hand. It was a big, strong, male-looking hand. 'No, to be sure it's not easy; more like it's simple. As soon as you believe in it, it becomes so very simple. And if you don't believe in it, it's not the smallest bit simple, or easy, or even possible.'

My turn to go, 'Ah!'

We exchanged looks and understood each other. But we weren't going to find the tomb that day because the sun was high and hot, there was no signal on Delyth's phone and the walk was going to be too long for safety without hats and water. Too many people these last years of a hotter and hotter planet had died just walking the way we were doing, so reluctantly we turned back.

'But we'll try again, for sure we will,' said Delyth.

'I'm just impressed that you are sensible enough to give up,' I said. 'I doubt without you that I would have been.'

? said Hero, slightly outraged as she had begun warning energies in my head that I had quietly been ignoring. Rus-El was just standing, staring at what looked like dust thrown up by a car in the distance. S/he was looking moodily magnificent and dusty pink. I was suddenly struck by the fluid-gender similarity between Rus-El and Delyth. And then I was struck at a completely different level by Delyth herself as she pushed me roughly behind a large rock.

'Down!' she hissed. 'That's not a car we want to see us, especially out here alone.'

Obediently I crouched behind the rock and then sat down as my knees were finding all this clambering and kneeling a bit challenging. I didn't say anything; I'd find out soon enough.

Hero made the sort of sound that indicates when a human puts both hands out, palms upwards and shrugs. It means something like IwastryingtowarnyoubutofcourseyoudidntlistentoME!

'Sorry!' I whispered to her.

Rus-El did not dive behind a rock. Rus-El was heading off towards the car. Given the various disasters that befell this angel every time it tried to defend me, I hoped whatever happened didn't hurt too much (do angels get hurt?)

No, destroyed, said Hero which was not entirely cheering.

Demons? I asked.

No.

Oh good. That *was* a relief.

Nothing happened; the car passed by and Rus-El spent some time apparently contemplating a lizard.

'Okay, let's head back,' said Delyth. She was obviously expecting me to enquire but I rather hoped it was none of my business.

'We're not exactly popular,' she said. 'At least, I'm not.'

'Orthodox folk?'

'Yes…' she hesitated. I tried not to sigh; it was obvious that she needed some reinforcement and vicars are meant to be good at that.

'You mean the sort who don't realise that the first chapter of Genesis makes it quite clear that God is feminine *and* plural? Effectively, the first "they/them." And that the Tetragrammaton isn't male or female but more likely a verb? And that we are made in the image of God, not God made in the image of what they want It to be?'

'Well there's a bit of that.' She gave me a wide smile 'but it's mostly "who do you think you are, trying to find the First Temple?"'

I was just grateful that it wasn't demons.

Back at base we all shared some more pickled meat and vegetables with olive bread, somewhat sweaty cheese and revolting own-brand canned cola under the slightly doubtful shade of a canvas awning. Then, hats firmly on heads, Delyth and Ali between them showed me around the entire site, highlighting the borders with the dowsing rods which followed traces of a building with four separate areas to it. That would accord perfectly with what we knew of the First Temple. There were areas already dug showing possibly fallen walls and entrances.

'What's particularly interesting is that there's really not a lot left of most of it—but here,' Delyth's L-rods crossed as she spoke, 'there's some kind of underground cavern. Definitely a source of water. It's beginning to look like the heart of this temple was either sunk by seismic activity or actually set either in caves or earth workings.'

My head spun. I guess up until this moment part of me hadn't fully taken on board that we were genuinely at the site of the First Temple. You can be as intellectually informed as you like but being present is a different ballgame.

It's deemed 'credible' by most archaeologists that artefacts found in this region had been removed from the temple site by Muslims and dumped in the Kidron Valley. Certain Muslim authorities have even claimed that the Temple Mount was an ancient mosque dating back to Adam and Eve and reject all claims that it was ever the site of a Jewish temple. And as no one may excavate at the Dome of the Rock, it's incredibly hard to prove anything definitively.

'Okay,' I said. 'What of the artefacts that were dumped round here—pottery, coins etc? Are any of them from the First Temple? I gather from what I've read that they are from the second temple but oddly the Internet isn't one hundred per cent reliable on that kind of thing.'

Delyth and Ali both made that 'poof' sound that means 'who the fuck knows?' but then they both folded their mouths.,

'So, there's something you'd like to tell or show me but you aren't sure if you should?' I hazarded.

'Kinda,' said Delyth. 'Ben will be back soon.'

Which he was. And quite shockingly in nearly normal clothes, by which I mean a polo shirt, chinos and a replacement hat made from woven palm leaves to shade The Nose. A baseball cap would have done a proper job but those were probably anathema. Even so, I hardly recognised him.

'Another wild goose chase,' he said as he got out of the battered old Land Rover. 'But every day we get closer.'

'What did you think it was?' I asked as I handed him a sweet mint tea. We had a kind of samovar which chugged away providing ridiculously hot drinks in a steaming climate but it boiled the water, sorting out any bugs and saving on plastic bottles.

'They *said* it was a papyrus that showed where the Ark of the Covenant was hidden,' said Ben, blowing on his brew, taking off his hat and pulling out an enormous white linen handkerchief to wipe his brow. 'I didn't believe that for a minute but they might have had information they didn't *know* they had. Sometimes you can trick those who want to trick you.'

'And did they want to trick you?'

'Oh yes! Everyone does. Rich foreigners coming to seek something in their land which they will almost certainly take away and which gives no benefit in return. Why would they not?'

'Because it's wicked,' said Ali, who was also pouring herself a cuppa.

'No, no,' said Ben. 'It's a kind of mental gleaning. You know what gleaning is, right?'

'That's different,' said Ali briskly. 'Gleaning is where you *leave* ten per cent of your crops for people to gather.'

'Have you ever gleaned, Ali?' asked Ben.

'No, of course not!'

'There's no "of course not" about it,' he said dryly. 'Anyone can be brought down to the level of subsistence.'

'I take it you have?' I said quickly in that ridiculous, vicary, way of jumping in to salve a tense moment.

'I have,' said Ben. 'Just a few times. And every single time I took more than was my due. I didn't see why I shouldn't. Does that make me wicked, too?'

'*How* did you take more than your due?' said Ali. 'If it was only the leavings in a field.'

'I took some from the field next door which hadn't been cropped,' said Ben.

'That's still not the same as wilfully tricking someone,' said Ali.

Ben sighed and absentmindedly handed me his mug to refill. Oddly, I didn't mind.

'St. Augustine pointed out that evil doesn't exist,' said Ben. 'Socrates posited that people act wrongly because they think wrongly; Plato taught that evil was purely an erroneous way of believing and had less power than most people think—but I shall quote Emerson directly:

'"God is positive. Evil is merely privative not absolute. Evil is like cold which is the privation of heat. All evil is so much non-reality."—wait!'

He put his hand up as both Ali and I tried to interrupt. Delyth sat with laughing eyes. She had obviously heard this before and was enjoying our reactions.

'There is a prevalent fervour of belief among the Jewish mystics that evil entered the world with creation. The Qabalistic tradition says that when God created the World He did it by filling vessels known as *sefirot* with light. The *sefirot* shattered because they could not contain that level of radiance. That created shards that are the source of evil.

'Christianity, of course, has the devil which is similar thing and *all* the religions have a dark-god aspect; the tempter, you might say. This *accuser* (which is what the word 'Satan' means) is there to challenge you to run before you can walk so that you fall over, feel shame and never try again. It's a winnowing tool.'

He paused to give us space to protest. Delyth put a hand on Ali's knee which (interestingly) silenced her, for the moment at least, and the big red-head looked at me with raised eyebrows which had the same effect.

'Go on,' I said. As someone who'd met a good few demons but

who was learning that love genuinely can overcome them, this was fascinating to me. No evil? Really?

'These great men knew that saying "no" to the appearance of evil dissolves the fear of it,' said Ben. 'As soon as you are not afraid of it, it has no power. If you fear it, it becomes real.'

'But what about earthquakes and what about 9/11?' said Ali who was now bubbling with frustration.

'Earthquakes aren't evil,' said Ben and I simultaneously.

'Thousands die in earthquakes!' said Ali.

'And that's not evil,' said Ben, patiently. 'That is a planet sneezing. I doubt there is a planet in the entire universe which does not sneeze in some way. It's a planet thing. What *might* be considered evil is when humans don't help people who are affected by natural disasters. But that brings me to my point. *All so-called evil is caused by human hate or fear.* There is no evil in whatever you want to call Spirit or Divinity but there is wrong thought in humans.'

'What about the Tree of Knowledge?' I said.

'What about it?' Ben swung towards me, frowning.

'*Towb* and *ra*,' I said. 'Hebrew for "good and evil"—the Tree of Knowledge of good and evil. Genesis chapter two.'

'I know where it is,' said Ben even more dryly. 'And was not the entire point that we should not eat from that tree?'

'Does humanity not eat from it every single day?' I countered.

Ben gave a bark of laughter.

'Indeed we do!' he said. 'And the occasional nibble can be helpful as in "is this suitable for me?" or "I'll leave that well alone." But judging things the way we do? Simply not on.'

'Try stopping us,' said Ali. 'Particularly now with the news the way it is and social media.'

'Precisely,' said Ben. 'We would rather be ruined than changed — good old W. H. Auden. So much easier just to get the dopamine hit or the outrage rather than doing something really crazy like travelling to Israel to look for the First Temple. But it is all choice. Lack of choice is in itself a choice. Yes—' he raised his hand again to stop me from interrupting. 'Choice is important but the choice is to make clear decisions not to regard something as evil because you don't approve of it.

'You don't eat pork,' he said to Ali. 'That's fine; your religion—and the orthodox version of mine as well—forbids the eating of pork. So don't eat pork. When you start scoffing from that tree you make everyone else wrong for eating pork and pretty soon the "wrong" are lesser than you and then "bad" and then "evil."'

'Particularly if they live on land you want or have resources that you want,' put in Delyth.

'And that's the evil-added-to-evil,' said Ben. 'The determination that *your* belief or decision is good and therefore you have the *right* to control the other's delusions and bully them into the true faith that is your own.

'Presenting something that is clearly evil, such as invading another country; killing civilians or denuding the land itself as being *good*. That's the ultimate evil.'

'Presenting gun culture as good,' said Delyth.

'Presenting authoritarianism as faith,' I said.

'Presenting building more houses for individuals as good when it damages the land instead of living in community,' said Ali.

'Ooh,' we all said in reply. That was a complex one.

'The human ego thinks it wants to live in community but it also wants to be led and told what to do,' said Ben. 'Most of us only want to live in the kind of community that *we* approve of. Is that community at all?

'But enough yatter!' he stood up. 'Where are we with the plans? Where are we with the next place to dig? Where are we? We can talk until we are blue in the face but we are here to find a miracle.'

'Talk to him about Bathsheba,' said Delyth quietly as we got up and sorted ourselves out to get to work again.

'You think?' I said.

'Yeah. He's a one for dreams.'

So I did. I followed Ben to one of the tents, where he was leaning over a table and reading something through fabulously old-fashioned half-moon glasses, his face shockingly raw with worry. The expression switched into his usual urbane one as soon as he saw me but I wasn't fooled and said so.

'So what's the matter?' I asked.

'Money,' he said, throwing his hands in the air. 'Supplies,

support, keeping the archaeological community behind us, dealing with the opposition to what we are doing. Of course you'd never for a moment suspect that the Hebrew nation would like to find their original temple and the possible solution to the Arab-Israeli problem of Jerusalem. Good God no! They'd rather get mired back down in some sort of persecution outrage—which, to be fair, is the same with all nationalities nowadays, But basically, it's money. If I could only find something to show people what we're doing is worthwhile, that would bring in the support we need.'

'Delyth and Ali think you have something you wanted to show me,' I said. 'Is that not "something" that we could show people?'

'No, it's not. At least not yet,' he said, magnificently failing to open up about what it might be.

'Okay…' I said slowly. 'Then what about Bathsheba's tomb?'

'*Bathsheba's tomb?!*' That was more of a bark than even an exclamation.

'Yes. I had a dream about it. One of those portentous dreams that asks you to find something and implies that you will.'

'Well, that could work!' Ben stood up straight, rubbing his back with both hands. 'Can you dowse?'

'Not yet.'

'Good answer.' He smiled at me. I noticed that he had one tooth slightly crooked. 'Then we'll start looking for that tomorrow. Now sit down and tell me all about that dream.'

'Are you my Anam Cara?' I thought. Hero was silent. 'How much dare I tell you?' I thought. Hero was silent. Silence usually means 'no.'

Oh well. I never listen; she just told me so. I took a big breath and began.

Chapter Fourteen

I DIDN'T TELL him everything; not about travelling with Jon and Sam and Callista, but I did tell him about the demon in St. Raphael's and the dissolving altar, about Bishop Paul's group of exorcists, about his murder, about the devil in the cathedral getting my name wrong, about the paedophile ring and about my beautiful hound from heaven who came to ask me to free the soul of her master. And I told him about Marcus. Well, a *bit* about Marcus.

It took more than an hour. Ben didn't laugh at me nor interrupt. Occasionally he asked questions and twice he said, gently, 'slow down' as I began to clutter my sentences as I realised how utterly preposterous it all sounded to an absolute beginner. But then, Ben had been able to see the invisible me so he *couldn't* be an absolute beginner.

'Fine,' he said when I had finally wound down. 'Let me see if I can sum all of this up. You had a head injury and since then you can perceive angels and demons—and ghosts. I still hold to the belief that your demons were all very human-inspired but we can agree to disagree on that point if you want. Everyone has a different reality and I'm not about to diss yours.

'I suspect that despite that incredible shedload-of-unloading you still haven't told me everything and that's understandable. Most medical people would try to section you on sight.'

I nodded, embarrassed to realise that tears were running down my cheeks.

'Fine,' said Ben again, very slowly. 'I have one main question.'
'Yes?'
'Are you aware, at any point, of having slipped into any other dimensions?'
'Yes. Often.'

'Good.' He took another enormous, linen, handkerchief out a pocket and handed it to me. 'This isn't to tell you to stop crying,' he said. 'I think there are a *lot* of unshed ears in you and they all deserve to flow. It is purely a gesture of solidarity.'

I gulped and fresh tears flowed. How many people in the world would have realised that, to so many women, the handing of a handkerchief generally meant 'stop fussing and clean yourself up'? And what did he mean by 'solidarity'?

My ego, briefly, congratulated me on my strange ability to cry beautifully without puffiness or undue levels of snot.

Then Ben leant back and blew out a long, long breath.

'One more question,' he said 'Have you, in one of those other universes, visited the First Temple in its own time?'

'Yes. I think so.'

'You *think* so?!'

'Yes, I have,' I amended. 'I can't explain how.'

'I doubt anyone could,' said Ben dryly. 'Very well. I'm going to show you something.'

He got up and pulled his laptop from a battered, soft-leather rucksack.

'I started out as a theoretical physicist,' he said. 'Loved it, of course. I could have spent many a happy decade researching and cataloguing the almost-inexplicable and doing nothing practical whatsoever. Then I was asked by a friend in archaeology if I knew anyone who could help them locate an ancient wooden temple through identifying tiny variations in the soil's magnetic field. There was no actual wood left, of course.'

He opened the laptop and started up a program.

'People assume that sacred places are built from stone. Stonehenge and all that. But much of it depended on your surroundings. For every structure that required enormous stones there would have been dozens woven in wood.

'Right. Come over here if you would.' He had put the laptop on the folding table where we ate our meals, sat down and pulled up a chair next to his. I sat. He smelled like brown treacle.

'Here's the line from Delyth's dowsing,' he said bringing up a diagram of the topography with a series of yellow lines depicting a building with four sections. It was pretty much identical to what she had shown me.

'And now, here's the magnetic report.' He hit another key and the most extraordinary thing happened. A series of lines and patches in purple and gold interposed themselves on the dowsed lines. At the outer edges which would have marked what we now call 'the court of the Gentiles', where anyone could go, they were fairly stable but as you moved into the centre, where presumably the Holy of Holies stood, they shimmered and then vanished. Nothing at all showed in the centre.

'The reading simply dies,' he said, pointing to the centre. 'You probably know that dark matter can't be read electronically?'

I nodded.

'And the only way we can detect it is through its indirect effects on gravity and its impact on areas which *do* have mass and light?'

I nodded again. I was bluffing but I wanted to hear what came next.

'Well, I'm pretty sure that is exactly what is here,' said Ben. 'The heart of the temple is pure dark matter. We won't be able to access it in this dimension. And that's why we need you.'

'But what *is* dark matter?' I said. 'Surely nobody knows?'

'Oh yes, we know,' said Ben. 'Even cynical agnostic physicists like me know what it is. We just don't want to admit it. Dark matter is the glue that binds the universe together. It is what most people call Spirit and what mystics call Divinity. It is what the Jedi call the Force. You would be wrong actually to call it "God" because it is impartial and most religions view God as decidedly partial.'

'God is love,' I said automatically. 'Well, to me, that is.'

'The Party Line. And God is retribution and judgement to others,' said Ben. 'But dark matter is the ebb and flow of life itself. On its own it explains the law of karma—push it and it rebounds.'

'So if you send joy into it, it repays the same?'

'Probably. But don't get started on any New Age nonsense.'

'I could quote at least six passages of the Hebrew Bible that teach that kind of what you're calling both karma and New Age nonsense,' I retorted. 'There is nothing new under the sun.'

'Interesting,' said Ben. 'One day we might examine that. But right now, we have a temple to uncover and given that we are pretty sure that we *have* found it and you are here and can find other dimensions, we need to know next what Bathsheba's grave has to do with it.'

'Hang on a minute,' I said. 'Are you telling me that the Holy of Holies of the First Temple exists—or existed—in another universe or dimension?'

'I don't know. It rather looks as though that's the only rational explanation but I somewhat suspect that there *is* no rational explanation.

'Bella, there's no rational explanation for anything you've told me today. But that doesn't mean it isn't true. What *is* true is that humans can only see less than one per cent of the light spectrum so it is *entirely* rational to assume that there is much, much more on all levels that we cannot perceive. Absolutely-bleedin'-obvious that most, if not all of it, appears to be in dark matter.'

'But hang on… if we—if I—find it and no one else can see or perceive it, what good is that?'

'And that's a very good question. I suspect we'll only know the answer when we find out,' said Ben. 'And that is definitely the most confusing reply I could give but the only available one to my brain at the moment. Shall we do just that? Find out?'

'I don't know if I can change dimensions at will,' I said reluctantly. 'When it happened, it just happened.'

'Cheer up,' said Ben. 'It might just happen again. And surely your next questions are going to be "how did you find me and how did you know to look for me?"'

'That had crossed my mind,' I said.

'You'd be an idiot if it hadn't,' said Ben reverting to acerbic type.

'I already knew about your book and Maisie told me about your trial and the tape that was played. That tape had quite a lot of audio of you speaking as though there were someone else there. Maisie was there in court. Didn't you know?'

'I didn't notice. I was rather distracted.'

'Yes, you would be. I applied to the court for a transcript and it certainly sounded like you were, at least, talking to another dimension. I thought it was worth a punt.'

My head was starting to spin and I excused myself to take some much-needed time out. I spluttered something and Ben nodded.

'Take your time,' he said. 'Take the Sabbath. And then come back and we will begin. There really is no going back from here, Bella, is there?'

'I guess not,' I mumbled and moved away.

This was Friday afternoon and we followed the Jewish custom of taking the Sabbath off from just before sunset to the sight of three stars on Saturday night. A custom that could only be invented in a land where you could reliably expect to see three stars every Saturday night but, even so, you can always follow the concept. It did feel odd to me to rest on Saturday and work on Sunday but technically that was ridiculous as I *always* worked on a Sunday. I've long considered it ironic that ministers of all religions are expected to lead people to God on the exact day of the week that God has requested a bit of peace and quiet...

I sat for a while in the open air, considering everything. I prayed a little for guidance. Yes, I have contact with angels but the Big Boss is always worth touching base with even if only to keep the lines of communication open, whether or not they come direct or via messengers.

The decision God/my intuition came up with changed my life forever. And yet, who knows? If you have a destiny do all roads lead there or not? Would there have been an alternative way? An easier one? Or maybe, God forbid, an even harder one?

I booked myself into another Airbnb for two nights just so that I could be on my own. I think Ali was pleased about getting some personal space, too, and she was more than happy to drop me off just inside the Damascus Gate into Jerusalem. I walked up to the Salesian Sisters Pilgrims' Home, checked in and found my way to a simple, en suite private room. The super-fast internet soon had a series of 'pings' going on my mobile and, to my utter delight, there was a message from Alessina who was back from hospital and staying in the Rectory. She wanted to know if I fancied a video call. Heck yes!

Lucie was requesting one, too, and she did say 'urgent!' but I put that off until the following morning. She messaged back in full autocorrect magnificence, 'I'll loofah your tit. Big jugs,' which I inferred probably meant 'I'll look forward to it. Big hugs.'

I had arrived in time to attend the daily Mass in the nearby Chapel of Notre Dame and as Jerusalem is two hours ahead of the UK I reckoned I should be able to fit in the call with Alessina, prayer *and* supper.

Of course, not being a Catholic, I didn't take communion physically but emotionally and spiritually it was abundantly available. I had a sudden surprise memory of a time at theological college when my class attended a Catholic Mass and the others were clearly upset that they weren't allowed to go up for the bread (no wine at this particular church, which is quite common in Catholicism). I just sat and imbibed the Spirit anyway and couldn't see the problem. I don't think I was terribly popular at theological college.

Communion is odd. Orthodox Christians take it as a given that it is transubstantiation of the body of Jesus Christ—thereby assuming that 'Christ' is basically Jesus' surname. Most non-Christians laugh at the idea of eating the body of Jesus or call it 'spiritual cannibalism' but it isn't the body of *Jesus,* it's the body of *Christ* and Christ (as Jesus said) existed long before Abraham. Christ is the God Force and in that beautiful line 'what Earth has given and human hands have made' for the bread and wine you have, what is for me, the essence. Christ is the meld of the human (him and now us) and the Divine (creation itself which, here, is embodied in all the Earth).

At least it is in my world…

I stayed in the chapel after the service, watching and listening. I'd seen the angel at the altar and acknowledged him (much to his surprise) and there were ghosts and echoes here from many, many years before. And I prayed. I asked for Grace and for healing and for patience and I asked to be shown the way to Bathsheba's tomb and to complete my destiny of finding the temple. And, if it were the will of the Holy One, to find the heart of the temple itself in what to my non-scientific mind was going to be some kind of black hole.

Would I come back if I did find it? Could I? And most importantly of all, was I (and was Ben) simply stark, staring mad?

A priest came up to me to ask if I would like to take confession. I felt like asking for extreme unction but I just smiled and politely shook my head.

'Bless you my child,' he said. He spoke in accented English because everyone in Jerusalem can spot a Brit or an American on sight.

'Thank you, Father,' I replied. 'I have an impossible project to undertake and I will need all the blessings I can get.'

'Use Mary as your backstop,' he said. 'Mother Mary will help you.'

He passed on and I continued to ponder-pray until it was time to go to talk with Alessina. On my way out, I looked up at the great statue of the Virgin and Jesus on the crenelated roof, crossed myself semi-automatically and felt—what did I feel? Indescribable but definitely a kind of connection.

No time to contemplate that and no time for supper as I had long overstayed my time in the chapel. Damn. Alessina would be waiting.

My poor dear friend did not look good. A big chunk of her lovely black hair had been shaved so surgeons could operate to repair her skull and she was both thinner and seemed even to have gone very slightly grey.

She was trying hard (and failing) to be positive and was simultaneously almost pathetically grateful for sanctuary in the house and utterly hating having to be there. I grieved for the (hopefully temporary) loss of her vitality and sympathised with her over the destruction of her beautiful home.

'They say there's structural damage,' she said. 'Up to a third has to be completely rebuilt. Our lovely, lovely home. And oh Bel, it wasn't insured.'

'Not insured? Not at all?'

'Yes, but apparently we had underestimated its value,' she said, bitterly. 'God knows how that happened. So it can't be restored in full. And I don't even know if I want it rebuilt. I don't even know if we want to stay here.'

'It's still very early days,' said the woman who knew quite a lot about head injuries. 'You can't be expected to know anything much. I know it's frustrating and horrible and I am so sorry. Have the police charged anyone?'

'They have.' She hesitated. 'Two people.'

'*Two* people?'

'Yes. That man, Norris and…' she paused.

'And?'

'Will,' she whispered, naming the formerly homeless man who had saved my life in the cathedral and who had become a born-again Christian and Lucie's boyfriend. And who, in a parallel universe, had committed a date-rape against me. And no, I hadn't warned either Alessina or Lucie that he might be that untrustworthy; how do you explain something like that? But I felt a huge rush of guilt as well as compassion for poor Lucie.

But that could wait.

'Shit,' I said. Because you have to say something. There was a pause.

'You have a home in the Old Rectory for as long as you need,' I said. 'And I mean it. You have plenty of time to decide. And it's a long road to getting better; you know that.'

'But you'll be coming home soon?' It was a hopeful question from the echo of my old friend.

'I don't know. Not for a good two months more. Plenty of time for this to work out somehow.' (*for both of us*, I thought).

'Why do you hate us so?' the witch asked the vicar, sadly.

'You know I don't.'

'You know what I mean.'

'Yes, I do know. Because you are powerful. Because "we" fear you. Because "we" have so little faith that another form of faith is a threat. Because you have a magic that so many of us don't. And I am so, so sorry.'

'I've lost my magic,' she said, head bowed.

I wasn't having any of that crap. Not from Alessina.

'Did you die, Alessina?' I asked.

'Yes. For a while.'

'And what was it like?'

'I didn't want to come back,' she said, simply. 'And I feel so guilty about that. I would happily have gone on and left Luke and the children.'

'But you *did* come back.'

'I came back for them… and for you.'

'Then you're an absolute prat for feeling guilty then, aren't you?' I said. 'You *did* come back even though you wanted to stay. There's no reason for guilt there.'

She smiled. 'I guess not,' she said. 'I'm not really myself.'

'Of course you're not. And yet you are,' I said. 'Darling, I do know a bit about what this is like and it's not easy. Your brain basically has to rewire itself. Do you want to tell me about that experience with death?'

'No,' she said. 'Not yet. It hurts.'

'Okay. Yes, I get that.' We held each other's eyes for a moment and Hero whispered, angel hurt and what sounded like re-boot.

'My guardian is saying that some of this is your own guardian needing time to recover,' I said, sounding lame even to myself.

'Huh,' she said, with a slight smile. Alessina did totems and allies rather than angels.

She wasn't well enough for me to share my own news and that made me feel, selfishly, lonely. I had come to rely on her love and good sense and now she needed to focus on her own healing.

We talked a little longer and I wished I could take her in my arms. As well as her own grief and suffering she had to handle Luke's (it was he who had been responsible for the insurance) and her children's distress. This was going to be a long road.

'Your house is lovely,' she said bravely. 'It made us very welcome.' So she hadn't lost her intuition; she could feel what she called the Spirit of Place. That was encouraging.

'And the villagers?'

'They're being very kind. And apologetic. Friends are bringing hot food. I don't have the co-ordination to cook yet and Luke isn't brilliant at it. I know this is what they call "a nine day wonder" but all the attention and the enquiries are quite tiring. But what about you, Bel?'

'I can wait. I'm fine. Go sleep and sleep and sleep again,' I said. 'This too shall pass. I promise.'

The call unsettled me (and here I am being selfish again because what were my problems compared with hers?) and I was hungry so I went out for some street food and to wander around the city.

Jerusalem is a place of wonder and of spasmodic terror. The bomb went off close enough to blow me off my feet and far enough not to maim or kill me. I was one of the lucky ones.

I lay choking on the street, only choking because my falafel had gone the wrong way and that was soon sorted. I had a grazed hand and bruised arm and felt half-deafened and disoriented from the noise. I scrambled up, leaving my half-eaten supper on the ground and moved forward to see if I could help.

NO, left! said Hero. This from the guardian angel who hadn't warned me about a bomb. She pretty well pushed me down the steps towards the Church of the Annunciation with the white Virgin Mary on its forecourt.

The statue raised her head and smiled at me. Her hands were held out towards me.

'Okay, I have concussion,' I thought, staggering slightly.

Mary opened her arms wide and engulfed me and I was inside of her.

Chapter Fifteen

THE WORLD WAS soft and filled with glory. A great spiral of pearl-like light drew me in and I half floated, half stumbled into what first impressions likened to a silken womb. A place of the feminine, for sure. Then it was a great folded passageway, as though I was being reborn and, oh wow! I could *see* Hero by my side. She was stunning; vibrant shades of green and gold with slanted turquoise eyes. Alien, definitely, but *my* alien.

I wasn't walking; I was floating.

'You're beautiful,' I said to Hero.

She bowed her head in acknowledgment of my intent. She didn't need the words; she knew what she was.

Trust, she said.

'Don't have a lot of alternative,' I replied and found myself tumbling downward through a kind of warm-but-dry steam. Visibility gone; no sound but a scent of roses.

Shouldn't it be lilies? asked my brain, without my consent.

That was courteously ignored. Angels don't do 'shoulds.'

Tumbling, bouncing from soft cushion to soft cushion, I lost sense of time and space.

'Maybe I'm being taken to Bathsheba's grave!' I thought when there was enough regrouping in my head to consider anything other than pedantics, the journey and the angel.

Splat.

I was sitting on the floor a cave; a court room almost with a dark, dark figure of a woman seated before me.

Justice, whispered Hero, still bright beside me.

Oh great.

She stood. And she must have been nine feet tall. All around her was black stone but she was clearly visible.

YOU CANNOT PROCEED BEFORE YOU HAVE DONE THAT WHICH

YOU LEFT UNDONE, she said in a voice as deep as the Atlantic Ocean.

Oh dear God… what have I left undone?

Probably quite a lot of stuff. Oh shit.

'Am I going to die?' I bleated.

Both angels looked at me as though I were a prize idiot.

ALL HUMANS DIE said Justice, with astonishing tact considering the gibbering idiot on the floor.

GO. COMPLETE THIS, she added.

And I was back in Exbridge on a bright, sunny day, sitting with the Dean on a rug with a picnic. And Margot was right beside me.

As I oriented myself, she pushed her nose under my hand so that I would stroke her and leant herself in to me.

Xander couldn't see her. He was talking and I realised it was five minutes before the advent of the Bishop. I could see a kind of whisper of the future where I got up and ran away. Obviously I had to do something different.

Margot nudged me again.

'Margot is with me,' I said, interrupting him.

Xander stopped dead. 'She is?'

'Have you wondered why she isn't with you?'

'I thought…' he stopped. 'Oh hell, I'm not clear, am I?'

'No, you're not clear. I thought you were, too, but you aren't.'

'Dammit!' he struck the ground with his hand. 'Yes, I can feel it now; like a weight around my head. Ow!'

He put his head in his hands.

'And you've arranged for the bishop to join us,' I said.

'Oh God, you must be a witch.'

'Not helpful,' I said sternly. Margot whined.

'Can you help?' said Xander.

'I really don't know,' I said. 'I have a friend who says that there is no external evil; it's all down to our misuse of free will. Maybe now you know it's there, you can set it free?'

'Where to? What if it goes into someone else?'

'I think we deal with that one when we get to it.' I sighed. 'Look, I'm going to try an open-air one-person exorcism. It's probably not the done thing but it's the only thing I can think of at the moment.'

'Go to it!' said Xander, hopefully.

I stood up, hoping against hope that everyone else in the park would be slightly hard of hearing.

Yes, said Hero.

Yes, said Rus-El

Yes, said another voice, presumably Xander's angel.

I blew out a big breath and began.

'In the name of Jesus Christ who holds power and authority over all evil,' I said and then began the Latin.

'Exorciso te, omnis spiritus immunde, in nomine Dei Patris omnipotentis, et in nomine Jesu Christ, filii ejus, domini et judicis nostri, et in virtute Spiritus Sancti ut descedas ab hoc plasmate dei Alexander Dubois, quod dominus noster ad templum sanctum suum vocare dignatus est, ut fiat templum dei vivi, et Spiritus Sanctus habitet in eo. Per eumdem Christum Dominum nostrum, qui venturus est judicare vivos et mortuos, et saeculum per ignem.'

'AMEN!' we chorused. And then Margot began to growl.

And he could see her.

The ghost dog leaped at her master's throat, her teeth closing on his jugular. Xander fell backwards and cried out and Margot was pulling something grey from the thoracic ganglion. She backed away growling as she pulled and, with the something fully out, she shook her head as dogs do automatically to kill their prey.

'Dear God,' said Xander, sitting up and clutching his throat. 'No! It's okay! Honestly!' he called to the two people who were staring at this strange and somewhat violent pantomime. Meanwhile, Margot kept on shaking and growling and backing away and whatever it was in her mouth was looking more and more ragged and darker by the minute.

Then there was a POP! And both of them were gone.

'Oh!' I said in horror. 'Margot!' But just as suddenly, Marcus was there.

'Befæsten' he said in Old English. 'Hæle.' The words were unfamiliar but the meaning clear. Margot was safe with him.

'Thank you,' I said with love. 'Thank you so much.'

He smiled and waved at me and was gone.

'Who was that?' said Xander.

'You could see him?'

'No, but you *were* talking to someone, yes?'

'Yes. He's a dog wrangler; takes care of their souls after death. Margot went to him and she is safe.'

'Oh, what a lovely job,' said Xander, visibly relaxing.

'Hello,' said the bishop appearing from behind a tree. And Rus-El was standing right beside me.

'Oh good—' I said, on purpose to gain myself some time.

No! Engage!

Hang on a minute, angels aren't supposed to interfere with human free will.

Not free will. Reaction. I am here. Protected.

Fair enough… and bugger. But… but… BUT! I was back in time and maybe I had time to warn Alessina?

Pause. And Rus-El (or someone) stopped time. Both X-Men were frozen still as were the rest of the people in the park.

You can only change your own destiny.

I ignored the angel. If it were my free will that Alessina's destiny changed, surely that counted? I pulled out my mobile phone and rang her number.

And she answered! Oh God, thank you so much!

'Bel, how are you? What can I do for you.'

'Alessina! There's a man—possibly two—coming to set fire to your house and one of them is going to throw a big stone through your work room window. I've seen it; it's true. I don't know if you can stop it but get out *NOW!* And call the fire brigade.'

'But… what…?'

Pause ending.

'Oh shit. I can't explain. Sorry. No time. But it's true! *Get out!*'

'Okay. I believe you.' And my amazing friend put the phone down.

I just had time to get my phone back in my pocket before a breeze rustled the leaves of the trees around us and everyone began to breathe again. I had to remember to breathe myself. Dear God, let me have been in time!

But back to the X-Men.

That old trope 'what doesn't kill you..' came into my mind and, out of the blue, Rus-El added, Disappoints everybody else.

My face creased in involuntary laughter so the first proper look the bishop had of me was of someone light-hearted and open.

'It's good to see you, Annabel,' said the bishop. 'Xander, you are looking well. May I join you?'

'Of course, Bishop,' said Xander, nervously. 'Most welcome.'

Jesus, he can't even get my name right!

He is bringing as much joy as a wet sock.

This time I was hard pressed not to snort out loud.

'Call me Xavier,' said Xavier sitting down cross-legged. 'I'm glad to find you both. A thought has crossed my mind.'

Must have been a long and lonely journey.

I folded my lips but they kept going up at the sides.

'Oh?' said Xander politely.

'Yes,' said Xavier.

(I do realise that this might get rather confusing).

'Well, I know that Annabel and I got off on the wrong foot so it would be lovely to start again and be friends.'

If he had an enema you could bury him in a matchbox.

I couldn't speak; I simply couldn't speak.

'You might want to call her by her true name if you want to improve your relationship,' said Xander bravely. 'It's *Am*abel, not *Ann*abel. It's French.'

'Oh! Well, of course, being a Dubois, you'd know that. Apologies *Am*abel!'

As useful as a waterproof tea bag.

'It's fine,' I managed to choke out. I wanted to be cross but I simply couldn't make it. 'Call me Bella, it's easier.'

Tell him you're sorry. Sorry for not slapping him twice; once on each face.

'I should apologise too,' I added, my face wreathed in smiles. Truly, I couldn't stop grinning.

'Thank you,' said Xavier. 'Friends, Bella?'

One day we'll look back on this, laugh nervously and change the subject.

'Absolutely!'

'So, what's this thought?' said Xander. 'Would you like a sandwich?'

'Thank you, no. I thought we could carve out a plan for when Bella gets back from her sabbatical.

My ears went back like an angry horse's but—

He changed his mind? Does this one work any better?

'…And?' said Xander.

'The diocese needs an exorcist. A deliverance officer, I should say,' said Xavier. 'The post has been vacant for a while now and although I don't personally believe in demons…'

It's impossible to underestimate him, isn't it?

'… I think it's something we should have.'

For a moment, I was interested. Surely no one experiencing possession would suggest such a thing? Maybe the bishop was fine now, after all. Or was it a cunning trap? And, if it were, could I come up with a cunning counter-plan?

Whatever is eating him must be suffering terribly.

That one broke me; I guffawed. Luckily I'd finished eating so I didn't spray cake in the bishop's face.

Then the world went weird again. Not exactly paused but I saw the bishop's angel wrap her arms around him and he began to laugh as well.

Xander, caught up in the energy, also laughed; the three of us in rocking back and forwards with joy together. I saw Rus-El and the guardian move around and into the bishop, bringing a cool and strong light down from above. Three frail wisps of energy emerged and dissolved into the brightness.

Hitchhikers not demons said Rus-El.

We were all down to that glorious stage of wiping our eyes and giggling and I knew already about hitchhikers.

Hitchhikers: Earthbound ghosts living on a human's life force. They suck energy and affect personality. Nasty ones. All gone now, explained Rus-El somewhat unnecessarily.

Can I go now, too? I want to get to Alessina in time.

Yes, go.

'Gentlemen,' I said. 'This has been delightful. And thank you,

Xavier, for that most thoughtful suggestion. May I think about it and get back to you? I'm heading off on a trip away tomorrow so I must get home and pack.'

I stood up and the world began to spin. I was falling though time and space.

'No, no, no, no! I have so much more to change!' I cried as I fell but to no avail. I landed back in the cave with Justice.

IT IS DONE, she said.

'What's done? All that happened was that I said hello to the bishop instead of running away.'

She looked at me as if to say 'that's my point.'

'But that was nothing! I could have done so much more. I might have saved my friend from harm; I might have stopped her house burning; I could have confronted Will.'

I began to cry tears of frustration. 'Did Alessina escape? What happened?'

CHILD, she said, putting me lovingly in my place. NO ONE MAY CHANGE ANY STORY BUT THEIR OWN.

'But I did nothing!'

YOU LAUGHED. YOU DISSOLVED ANIMOSITY. YOU HELPED HEAL.

'And that was all I needed to do?'

ONE THREAD UNTANGLED ALLOWS OTHERS TO UNRAVEL. LET IT BE.

'But why do I get to untangle something if nobody else does? Or does everyone get a chance to review and change things when they die?'

YOU ARE NOT DYING.

'Even so…' I can't believe I'm arguing with an aspect of the Holy One—because that's what I was pretty sure she was.

She didn't answer but C. S. Lewis's words through Aslan rang in my head: 'I am telling you your story, not hers. No one is told any story but their own.'

I didn't like it but I understood.

'What now?' I asked as politely as I could manage.

YOU WILL BE SHOWN THE TOMB OF BATHSHEBA AND FROM THERE YOU WILL FIND THE TEMPLE. NAME WHAT YOU SEE. DO NOT HESITATE. NAME WHAT YOU SEE.

Oh nothing enigmatic then...

Come whispered Hero and the world began to spin again.

I came to myself in the street of chaos with the sound of sirens and panic. Of course; there had been a bomb. Probably only a few moments ago. My hearing was muffled and my grazes hurt but I was okay, albeit torn between the desire to help and the urge to run away in case there was more savagery to come.

Staggering up, I moved towards the chaos but Hero diverted me.

Not your job she said.

Oh Jesus... but there were people there who were suffering. I could see them lying on the street or staggering or sitting.

You are not a doctor. Not your job.

She was right. I wanted to help but I would be horribly in the way of those who knew what they were doing. Guiltily, I turned away and limped back to the convent. I showered off dust and dirt, clambered into bed, curled up hugging a pillow and slept.

Chapter Sixteen

I WAS UP and out being a tourist of carnage at first light. I'd already checked the local news online and was relieved to see that no one, apart from the suicide bomber himself, had been killed and there were no mentions of 'life-changing injuries' but I still felt called to be there, to lament and to pray.

Hero walked/floated beside me. She was quite happy at my choice of occupation and, once I was in the street where the blast had blown in windows, destroyed a couple of cars and left dark stains on the ground, I halted before the police tape. There was a ghost there and it was the bomber.

He was so very young; hardly an adult at all. Presumably radicalised into believing that he would go straight to heaven for what was, at least, attempted murder.

He was already murdered, said Hero and I got it. Psychologically, this boy's whole life had been taken from him.

No, I didn't condone what he had done but I felt great pity for the stupid waste of it all.

'Can I help him?' I asked.

Draw down light around him. Call his guardian. Bless him.

I closed my eyes and visualised light flowing down around and through the boy, saw an angelic presence descend and wrap its wings around him—

'Jesus wept, woman! When were you going to have the fucking basic decency to let us know you were all right?'

The voice was harsh and loud and I was grabbed by the shoulders, turned and literally shaken. It was Ben. He had a right to be angry; it had never occurred to me to phone him and, to be frank, given the lack of signal at the site it would probably have been fairly pointless. But I didn't appreciate his method of approach.

'You could at least have left a message for me to pick up on the way in!' he scolded, reading my mind.

'It's 6am,' I defended myself. 'I didn't know you were awake.'

I was hedging and we both knew it.

'Sorry,' I added.

'You're not alone now, you know,' he said, still furious and holding me by the shoulders but at least being static about it. 'This is not the "no one cares about Bella show" any more.'

'Okay, I said I'm sorry. And that hurts.' I pushed his hand off my left shoulder which was bruised and scraped.

Ben took my chin in his hand instead and looked hard at the graze on my cheek.

'You're hurt,' he said accusingly.

'I'm not your toy. Let go!' I said. 'Yes, I'm scraped and bruised but I'm all right.'

'You were here when it happened?'

'Yes.'

'Oh my God. Get your stuff and let's hightail out of here.'

'No, I have a Zoom call with my assistant. Her boyfriend has just been arrested for arson and attempted murder back in Devon. She needs me.'

'*She* needs *you*? She's dating a murdering arsonist? What she *needs* is her head examined!'

'You're impossible!'

'True.'

Then he kissed me and, to my total surprise, I melted.

No! I will *not* fall for a vintage-clothes-dressing arrogant asshole who has the sensitivity of a decomposing sheep.

'Let me go! You have no right!'

'And you have no right to be so exasperatingly beautiful and so reprehensibly adorable. Yes, I'll let you go but at least now we know where we stand.'

'You may. I don't.'

'Do you have time for breakfast before comforting your idiot assistant?'

'She's not an idiot. I didn't warn her.'

'Then you are both idiots. Have you had breakfast? And how

could you warn her? Did you by chance *know* he was a murdering arsonist?'

'*Alleged!*' I said half-furious and half starting to find all this worryingly funny. 'No, but I did know he had the potential to be a rapist.'

'Oh right. And you didn't warn her about that?'

'It's complicated,' I said, sheepishly.

'Other dimensional?'

'Yes.'

'Right. Fair enough, that *is* complicated. All the same, she can bloody well wait. You've got your phone on you? She can call while we're eating. *I* need some protein and we *both* need coffee.'

'I don't like coffee,' I said, childishly.

'Did I say "like"?'

'Stop railroading me!'

'Shan't!'

We both started laughing and, despite my better judgement, ended up walking arm in arm to a café where we ate *Shakshuka*: eggs poached in a shockingly spicy tomato, onion and garlic sauce and served with *Ka'ak Al-Qud* ring-bread. We drank the kind of coffee that removes your taste buds, redesigns your stomach and challenges your liver to a cage fight. We did it all in a companionable silence as though we had been married for a dozen years.

Lucie texted just as I was swilling down a large glass of water which completely failed to alleviate the spices or remove the taste of the coffee.

Ben sighed as I took my phone from my pocket.

'Look, I have to go. I do have to take this.'

'Five minutes,' I texted back in reply to, 'Highball, are u three?'

'I'll wait. I've got the car. We've got all day. Don't be too long, there's stuff we have to do.'

'She's in trouble.'

'Yes, the kind you can do absolutely nothing about.'

'You are a heartless bastard.'

'Yes I am. Deal with it.'

He kissed me on the cheek as we left the café. I hurried back to the convent, redolent with mixed feelings.

Lucie could never look anything but beautiful but she was not at her best, poor girl.

'Alessina told me about Will,' I said as soon as we are connected. 'But tell me yourself too.'

It all flooded out. There was so much more than the torching of Alessina's house. And it was all so shockingly banal. I'd suspected Will was somewhat of a control freak when he first went at me for being friendly with a witch and started to assume that he had some right of way in my life. But I hadn't expected there to have been a problem with Lucie; she wasn't contrary like me and they'd always seemed in perfect harmony. In public at least.

And the date-rape between him and me had been in a parallel universe so how could I tell her that in another galaxy far, far away, her boyfriend's doppelgänger was the sort of man who would drug a woman's drink in order to have sex with her?

But I should have. Somehow I should have worked out a way.

This is not about you.

Hero's voice brought me up sharp. She was right; I was forgetting to listen and what Lucie needed was a listener, not someone obsessed with themselves.

I listened and comforted for half an hour. It was the least I could do. I knew she was worth better; I knew there were plenty more fish in the sea but she felt so hopeless and lost.

'I thought I loved him,' she wept. 'And I thought he was right about the arils. She did nearly poison us.'

'I don't think that was Alessina. I think that was Mrs Tiggy's grandchildren and a stupid joke.'

'Oh no! It must have been her.'

'Lucie…'

'Sorry, sorry. I thought he was right. I thought he was lovely.'

Yes, I had thought he was lovely too. And he had saved my life. I would always be grateful for that.

'He's been remanded in custody,' she said. 'I don't know whether to go and see him or not. Oh Bel, I don't know what to do!'

'Dump him and run for the hills' wasn't going to hack it so I simply said, as gently as I could, 'This is a safeguarding situation,

Lucie. You're a minister; I'm afraid you have to distance yourself from anyone who is deemed to be any kind of threat within the parish. You are the one people have to feel safe to come to and they won't feel safe if you're still associating with someone accused of attempted murder.'

'But what if he's innocent?'

'It's still what you have to do. It's in the regulations,' I said. 'I'm really sorry but you have to put the rest of the parish first. Do you think he's innocent?'

She hesitated and swallowed hard. 'I don't know,' she said.

'You do know that he has become very right-wing evangelical,' I said. 'From what you've told me he's very controlling; you say he thought Alessina was trying to poison us and I know myself that he thought she was the spawn of Satan.'

'And so did I,' said Lucie in a very small voice.

'Only for a while,' I said. 'You came to realise her value. She needs you, too.'

'She does?' Lucie looked surprised.

'Of course she does. She's a parishioner in trouble. She's lost her home and all her possessions. I think you can help each other.'

'She won't want to talk to me.'

'Whyever not?'

'Because I'm associated with Will.'

'Oh Lucie!' I tried not to show my impatience. 'Another good reason for walking away from him, yes? And you didn't support him in doing this—did you?'

'You think he's guilty!'

'I don't know what he is,' I said, feeling tired. 'I just hope you didn't support him emotionally if he was accusing Alessina.'

She was silent. So she probably had. Okay…

'Lucie, listen. This is important. Guilt is a very destructive emotion if you don't do something positive about it. Go and see Alessina and her family. See what you can do to help them. Being pro-active in trying to sort this out is the best thing any good human could do.'

'All right,' she said. 'I will.'

'You are a good, brave woman,' I said. 'I do have to go now as

Ben is waiting for me. I'm in Jerusalem at the moment and I have to get back to work.'

'Yes of course. Thank you Bel. Bye.'

Either she hadn't seen the news or she was so self-obsessed it never occurred to her to ask if I were okay. I hoped it was the former but actually, I didn't really care. That sounds really harsh but I was revved up for the next stage of the quest for Bathsheba's tomb and the First Temple. Maybe I was crazy but this crazy lady was stepping up and out.

And Ben was waiting. Impatiently, no doubt. I did a quick call to Alessina as I packed up my bag and she answered. Was it me or did she look a little better than last night?

'I have an odd thing to ask,' I said. 'Did I manage to warn you about the fire?'

'Yes, of course you did!' she said. 'Why are you asking?'

'Because I hadn't warned you and I got the chance to re-live that part of my life.'

'Bella! That's weird even for you. Yes, you did warn me—just in time. If you hadn't, it could have been so much worse.'

'But you still have a head injury?'

'I do. But I called the fire brigade as soon as you called. They got to us in time to save the house. Turns out we weren't fully insured so had it been worse we would have been in terrible trouble.'

'So it can be repaired?'

'Yes. Blimey. Were you in a world where it couldn't?'

'Briefly, yes.'

'Phew.' My friend blew out her cheeks.

'And how's your head?'

'Well, not that good but it'll heal and I'm mostly compos mentis. It was quite a close call, though. I am *so* glad you called. And I'm so grateful to be here in your home. Thank you.'

'My pleasure. I'm so glad. Have to go!'

Obviously she hadn't seen the news either. I think I can let Lucie off the hook. Let's face it, it *isn't* all about me.

Instead of waiting impatiently and telling me off for being so long, Ben was sitting on a kerbstone sharing some sticky lollipops and talking in Hebrew to three children. One of them was in his arms, sucking her sweet, and the other two were yabbering nineteen-to-the dozen telling him all about how their home had been filled with dust after the bomb and how scary it had been. Having just been talking about safeguarding I was surprised to see him with children who were strangers, and slightly concerned that it might be a problem, but then one of them called him 'Uncle Ben' so it was obvious he knew their family. I stood and watched as this arrogant, irascible man listened and comforted and made the little ones laugh. He was odd—but most of us are odd.

I liked him. There was no future in any relationship, obviously, because I was the one with the final exit plan but it was nice to feel something even remotely sexy again. My brain was going 'seriously?' but my other internal organs were doing that other strange thing a bit like a caterpillar going gooey in a chrysalis. It was entirely likely that I was starting to fall in love.

Neither of us said a word about the kiss. It's also entirely likely that we were both slightly in shock. But he had bought me a bunch of flowers which felt strangely appropriate in these rather weird circumstances.

We escorted the children back to the flat above their parents' shop where they lived. It had windows blown in but very little other damage. I was impressed by the stoicism shown by the people clearing up. And I'm not blind to the irony of the residents of one of the world's most sacred cities being totally used to war. The horrific Israel-Gaza crisis was still fairly fresh in most memories.

Then we spent most of the day in Jerusalem and Ben told me the whole story of what he rather amusingly called his 'morganatic marriage' to Maisie.

'We were very distant cousins,' he said. 'Only met a couple of times but she wanted a power of attorney and she couldn't stand that daughter of hers so she asked me. And then, given that I'm Palestinian in nationality—'

'You're what?'

'A Jewish Palestinian. We do exist. Anyway, Palestine never signed the Hague Convention of 1961 so Power of Attorney wouldn't be legal.'

'Well you live and learn!'

'Hopefully you do. So we got married, just in name. Just in case she needed someone outside the family for her legal affairs. She was considering disinheriting Connie.'

'That would have been unfair.'

'Yes, and I dissuaded her. She did give me money, by the way, but it was for trying to preserve some relics in Afghanistan, not for me.'

'And you were able to get married, online, via Utah even though you weren't even in the same country?'

'Yes. Look, I'll show you.' He brought out his tablet and did just that.

The world is a very strange and sometimes unexpectedly extraordinary place. And so is Ben Fairfax.

'What happened to the monocle?' I asked later on, when we were driving back to the camp.

'That's a magical artefact I found in a Victorian tomb,' he said. 'It can show ghosts.'

'Are you messing with me?'

'It is fair to say that I use it mostly to disconcert people but no. You of all people know how much magic there is unacknowledged in this world.'

I did indeed.

Our talk turned to work. What good would finding the original First Temple really do for two nations who simply couldn't realise they were family and could share? I asked.

'Who knows,' said Ben, negotiating his way around a tourist bus. 'But if we *don't* find it, nothing changes. And insanity is doing the same thing over and over and expecting a different result.'

I couldn't argue with that.

We got back to find that Delyth was bubbling with excitement.

'I think I've found the location of Bathsheba's grave,' she said. 'The rods were pretty specific. Bel, I hope you don't mind but I carried one of your scarves with me; it's good to have what we call a "witness" to dowse and you're the one with the link to the grave.'

'I wouldn't go that far,' I said.

'Well I would!' said Delyth. 'The rods were a lot clearer when I had your scarf in my pocket.'

'Is it far?' Ben gave her a clap on the back which would probably knocked me over but Delyth just grinned.

'About half a mile,' she said. 'And it's not the only grave; might be a few other royals around, too.'

'And how deep?'

'Probably five to ten feet. About a five-day dig, I'd say,' said Delyth.

'Only five days!'

'Well, to find *something*. After that we keep digging until we stop finding stuff. Given that there are up to three hundred micro-earthquakes here every day, the past gets very haphazardly buried.'

'Three *hundred* micro-earthquakes?'

'Yep. This is part of the Great Rift Valley that extends down into Africa. Not entirely stable land. They're way overdue another biggie right now.'

'Oh thanks!'

'Relax. You're here. God is on our side.'

God doesn't do sides, but I didn't bother saying that. Instead, I said, 'When can we start?' I was just *so* excited.

'No time like the present!' said Ben. 'Is everyone here?'

They were. We went into the covered meeting area where I was chaffed for deciding to go and have a restful Sabbath right next to a suicide bomb but that was good; it meant that I was accepted.

First step was magnetometry, scanning the area by computer, and that was fascinating. It looked as though there would be a passage underground and quite a large cave where hopefully Bathsheba had been buried—and perhaps others, too?

We were incredibly lucky in that the location was right on the edge of the area where we had permission to dig, from our permit from the Israel Nature and Parks Authority and the excavation license from the Israel Antiquities Authority, so we could go ahead and start. Ben did send them a message, as a matter of courtesy but, given that he hadn't actually told them that he was looking for the First Temple in the first case— '*So* many complications and *so* much opposition,' he said. 'Always better to go ahead and do what needs to be done and apologise afterwards.'

'Not *always,*' said Ali who was easily the most pragmatic of us all. 'Hitler didn't even apologise afterwards.'

Ben just looked at her over his nose. And when you got looked at by Ben over his nose, you stayed looked at.

'So what *do* they think we are looking for?' I said, looking up from the first trench and wiping my sweaty brow with the back of my hand.

'Tombs,' said Ben, cheerfully. 'Any possible important tombs. And if—*when*—we find this one then it'll be even easier to get financial support for going on. The main temple could take us a lot longer than we expect.'

Except it didn't.

We started out first thing the following day after a somewhat heated argument before going off to bed. Ben insisted that we all made wills.

'But I've already got one!' I said, part of a general chorus of protest.

'I don't care. We'll do it again. I'm not saying we are facing danger but just to be sure.'

Three of us refused outright, citing previous, much more legally-termed documents back home but even so, there were six handwritten, correctly termed and signed wills in the strong box before we left.

We found an access point to the passageway that the laptop had intimated in just three days. It was about three feet below the surface of the land and blocked off by a great square stone which had once been engraved but with what, we couldn't tell. Ninety per cent of the writing was unintelligible. There was the remnant of what might have been a carving of a tree—or even, perhaps, of a menorah. Jakob, our languages expert, thought he could spot some early Hebrew and he and I did our best to find some meaning in the faded markings but the stone was too worn.

We left it until the following morning to attempt to lift the stone but that evening we were all buzzing with excitement. Asher picked up a takeaway supper and we sat around an improvised fire pit and shared stories and even a little music. Malin and Jakob had a guitar and some bongos and sang in Hebrew and English with voices that chimed beautifully together. The rest of us joined in when we could and we drank a lot of cola. There was beer but no one wanted to be anything else than at the top of their game the following day.

Ben and I didn't have any time together to talk and he didn't seem any different from before. I didn't mind; if there was a spark, it was definitely less important than the incredible discovery we were hoping to make.

That night I dreamt again of the church and the snow and the angels. But this time my memorial stone had a slightly different name and a completely different date. I was 'Bella Ransom Fairfax' and had been granted another decade of life. It was a lucid dream so I was able to ask Hero what was actually true.

Fluid, she said. Three possibilities.

Then the image changed and the stone reverted to my familiar name and the date was less than a week away…

I woke up seriously pissed off. It was bad enough being told *one* death date without having the option of three. But whatever was going on, the worst-case scenario apparently was that I only had five days to find the First Temple of the Hebrews, so I'd better get a move on.

David, Isa and Malin stayed behind working on the existing dig. They didn't seem particularly bothered but then they weren't religious or even spiritual folk so this was simply another dig to them.

Mo, Jakob, Delyth, Ben, Ali and I had raised the stone by 8am, revealing steps down into a long, dark passage. I'd expected everyone to want to scramble down immediately but I guess they had all had seen enough movies where the intrepid archaeologist narrowly escapes the trap, mainly because the person who went in first, didn't.

So I went. After all, this was one of those days where I wasn't supposed to die.

I had a powerful torch and a rope tied around my waist with more being fed out by Delyth just in case the tunnel turned into a shaft. Ben followed behind me with Ali and the others, bless them, waited impatiently.

The tunnel was steep and long, occasionally stepped, stuffy, cobwebby and skittering with the noises of disturbed creatures. Probably nothing larger than a rat but it was unsettling all the same.

'Good sign. If there's nothing to eat, there's no life,' said Ben, happily. 'All corpses feed life and that life keeps on surviving wherever it is—what is it, Bel?'

I had stopped. Before me there was the dark glistening of water. We were at the edge of a small cavern with what looked like a lake. On either side of the wall entering the cavern were sconces with what might be tarred heads for lighting and, before us, was the skeleton of an old wooden boat.

'Damn,' said Ben. 'We'll need an inflatable and life jackets.'

Go round, from Hero.

'Hang on,' said Mo, 'this water has receded—see? It once used to be up to the edge of the tunnel. We might be able to wade. We could certainly test it out for depth.'

'I'm not sure we even need to,' said Ali. 'Over here!'

She was shining her torch on what could be a small doorway inset deep into the rock. Something glowed an odd kind of green in the bright focused light.

'Copper?' she said, leaning in and running her fingers over it. 'Yes. A lot of patina but still sound. And there is writing. Old Hebrew, I think, but it's very faint.'

Ben, Jakob and I moved forward and touched the door, too, as though we couldn't quite believe it was real.

'That looks a lot like *Gebira*,' said Ben. 'Which can mean Queen Mother. And that just could be *Malk* — maybe King or Queen.'

'They didn't use *Malkhut* that early,' said Jakob.

'Ah. But look! *Bet-Tav-Shan-Bet; B-th-sh-b,*' read Ben tracing the faint lines with his finger.

I felt a frisson of excitement down my spine and my throat choked up. It's one thing to believe and another to have evidence.

I stepped back while the others examined the little door more carefully to see if it would open. It was only about four feet tall and, obviously, very stuck in place. It was possible that no one had been here for more than two thousand years.

'Please let us open it,' I prayed, and found myself stepping forward. Ben and Ali wriggled out of the space to give me room and I felt Hero take my hand and guide it to what was probably once the door lintel. There was some kind of contraption there which looked and felt all the world like a bell-push.

So I pushed it.

The door opened.

Chapter Seventeen

WE CREPT THROUGH, bent double as though we were bowing which seemed very appropriate.

Inside, it appeared to be an oblong chamber about as big as those knocked-through downstairs rooms in a British Victorian terraced house. Just like Jon's and my house…

There were more sconces either side of the door and Jakob asked, in a gesture, whether he should light one with a match?

We all shook our heads. Nobody wanted to speak out loud; we needed to stand for a moment and take it in.

Our torches swept around the area, catching the glitter of what was either more copper or gold on the walls. It was remarkably dry and there were two sarcophagi—or, at least, extremely large, carved stone boxes which appeared to have no tops to them. Around the edges were human bones, in piles. Obviously this had been an ossuary as well as a tomb. We could only hope that it had been sealed soon after Bathsheba's death otherwise she, too, would just be a pile of unidentifiable bones.

Breathlessly, we moved as one to the first sarcophagus.

'Wooden lids,' whispered Ali. 'Only traces if the inlay left, look.'

But we were looking inside. Yes, there was an ancient skeleton with a gold circlet on its head and the vague shreds of some kind of robe or shroud.

'Nathan,' whispered Jakob who was tracing some old and faded Hebrew carving in the side of the stone.

'The prophet?' said Delyth.

'Bathsheba's youngest son,' I whispered and found tears coming into my eyes. 'She had four with David, four that lived, that is: Shammua, Shobab, Nathan and Solomon. Oh my goodness…'

We stood around the sarcophagus silently for a few moments.

'Shall we?' asked Ben.

'A moment,' I said, pointing my torch at the wall where something glistened.

It was a golden menorah inlaid into the stone. Each segment separate with all the knops and buds of the original.

'Oh wow.' We all just stood and stared. Then, we looked at all the walls around us. Ten Menorot, all gold.

'Fuck!' whispered one of us. Possibly more than one of us. There was an embarrassed silence and then we all simultaneously took in a deep breath and blew it out again.

'This is the real deal,' said Ben unnecessarily but totally understandably.

He led the way to the farther sarcophagus. Again, a wooden top with barely anything left but some golden freckles and—what was it? Lapis Lazuli? Yes, shards of it, dozens of them scattered all over the body which lay within the tomb.

Somehow she hadn't decomposed, like some of those amazing peat bodies you sometimes see. The body was dry and brown and the eyes were gone but greying black hair flowed out from her skull and her crown—oh my God, her crown!—looked like light itself. It was delicate crystal, carved into leaves and flowers and shone gold and silver in the torchlight.

In her crossed arms was what looked like a spatula in bronze. At her feet was another staff, short but also bronze. Tears sprang to my eyes.

'The sceptre will not depart from Judah, nor the ruler's staff from beneath her feet, until Shiloh comes, and to her shall be the gathering of the people,' I whispered, slightly amending Genesis 49:10 for a woman.

I said it because this woman was holding the sceptre of the God, El, and her feet rested on the 'lawgiver' staff. This was definitely the First Temple tomb of a queen and I was sure she must be Bathsheba.

Mo and Ali were now trying to find an inscription. Ben and Delyth were examining the crystal crown, Jakob was looking again at the Menorot on the wall. His mouth was wide open in wonder. I saw the tiny moth fly in and he began to cough.

The reverence of the moment shattered as he coughed and choked and spluttered. Delyth patted and then smote him on the back as he began to gasp for air.

'What the hell…' Ben tried the Heimlich manoeuvre but Jakob simply retched and coughed again.

And then there were more moths… seemingly a deluge of moths. Instinctively, I put my hand over my nose and mouth.

Run! said Hero. You cannot help. Run!

Delyth grabbed my arm and pulled. She had wrapped a scarf around her face and had Ali, who had pulled her hijab up over her nose and mouth, by the hand. We ran. It sounds cowardly but there you are.

The moths didn't follow us out of the room so, once we were back by the lake we checked ourselves over, wound what material we had more tightly round our faces—Delyth, bless her, tore her scarf in half with those strong hands and bound it round my nose and mouth for me—and holding hands, made our way back.

The men were all lying on the floor of the chamber. Dead? No, but unconscious and breathing shallowly. The moths had vanished.

Strangely they didn't return.

With shaking hands we checked the airways of all three men. Their mouths and noses were partially blocked by small, dead moths which we pulled out as best we could with our fingers. I think they were brown moths but we only had torchlight so it was hard to tell. I only cared because it might be relevant when—*if* —we got the men to hospital.

We checked pulses, which seemed relatively normal, and breathing which definitely improved as we cleared airways. We pulled up their eyelids but shining torches into their eyes didn't make their pupils change. They appeared to be comatose.

Delyth thought she might be able to carry one of them out but we would have to leave at least two behind.

'Is that your curse?' said Delyth to Bathsheba's sarcophagus. 'And is it only for men? If so, why not me?'

'Because your soul is that of a woman,' I said. Our eyes met.

'If it *is* that,' she replied. 'But how could that be? It's not possible.'

'We have no idea what is possible,' said Ali. 'But we must get help. One of us should stay behind...'

You, said Hero, just as I said, 'Me. I'll stay.'

'We need to drag them out of the tomb,' said Delyth. 'This is our discovery; it would be disastrous to have paramedics and police pounding in here.'

'But you shouldn't move bodies,' said Ali.

'They're *not* bodies,' said Delyth. 'It's not a crime scene either.'

'Let's take a breath,' I said. 'They don't seem to be in imminent danger.'

Ali passed round her water bottle and, carefully, we unwound our scarves and drank.

'It must be a curse,' said Ali. 'But how would you set that up?'

'High magic,' I said. 'It happened; it has to be possible.'

'I guess.'

We sat for maybe five minutes, absorbing the day's events.

'What if there's more to come?' said Delyth.

'Then there's more to come,' I said. 'But we can't just leave them.'

'Right,' said Delyth. 'I reckon I can carry Mo. If you're sure, Bel, we'll pull them all out to the edge of the water. Ali, would you leave your water with Bel? Stupidly, I didn't bring any.'

'Ben has a bottle of water on his belt,' I said. 'You take yours; you might need it on the way up.'

'No,' said Ali. 'We don't know how long we'll be. You might need both.'

'I suppose this might be drinkable, too.' I looked at the lake water.

'I'd wait for an analysis before thinking about even sniffing it.' Delyth pulled a couple of energy bars out of her pocket. 'We'll leave you everything we can. It will almost certainly be a few hours before we are back with help.'

In the end, I had three energy bars, some chocolate, a packet of boiled sweets and two spare watches ('you never know when the buggers will stop,' said Delyth) and three bottles of water. They left me four torches as well and I kept some matches I found in Jakob's pocket in case I needed to try and light a sconce.

I could hear Delyth grunting as they made their way back up the passageway, Mo dangling over her shoulder. Jakob and Ben lay neatly on their backs by the entrance, far enough from the water so that if they stirred they would stay dry. I sat down to wait. I suspected that Ben had broken his nose when he fell after losing consciousness; it was bloody and swollen. It looked like a giant boil on his face, poor man.

And now it begins, said Hero.

'What begins?'

The ending.

Oh thanks.

Cross the water.

'No, I'm going to wait for the others to come back.'

Cross the water.

Why?

Listen.

There was the sound of rumbling from the tunnel.

Cross the water. NOW!

Clouds of dust started rolling out into the cavern. I could hear falling rock. Oh shit, this was not good. Surely not an earthquake? But why not?

I leapt up and took a couple of steps, wading into the dark lake. Dammit! What about Ben and Jakob? And what about Ali and Delyth? Had they got out?

Rocks started rolling into the cavern. The noise was thunderous.

People float, don't they?

I grabbed Ben by the shoulders and heaved him with me into the water. It was pretty shallow at least for the first few metres so I was able to float him away from the rapidly-increasing pile of rubble.

I turned back for Jakob just as the roof of the tunnel fell in. He was lost underneath a ton of rock within seconds. And more was coming.

'Oh fuck!' I raced back into the water and pulled Ben further out and further and further. Jesus, it was cold! My brain started yelling, 'hypothermia!' but there was little choice. It was die here and now or risk dying later. Once it became too deep, I cursed again and wasted some valuable seconds pulling off my boots and trying to tie them round my neck with the laces. I dropped the torch but, thank God! It seemed waterproof and I was able to snatch it up again before it hit the bottom. Then I slipped and fell and Ben's comatose body turned over so there were several moments of absolute panic while I scrabbled on the slippery bottom with my socks, tried to right him to check he hadn't got water in his lungs and then swim on my back pulling him with me. I vaguely remembered those life-saving lessons that Jon had *made* me take thirty years ago.

'Thank you,' I sent up to him as I used my legs in a kind of bum-down breast stroke and pulled Ben further away from the still-falling rubble. The air was thick with dust and my nose was starting to fill up.

Once we were in the middle of the lake I stopped, sneezed non-stop for a good minute while I trod water; but in all my clothing and with boots round my neck it was horribly difficult, so I lay back again and kicked, my face covered with snot and hoping to God that I was going in a relatively straight line.

I have no idea how long I swam but it felt like even longer. Every now and then I tried to reach down with a foot to see if there was rock beneath me and, eventually, there was. Coughing, I tried to stand up, slipped and dropped the torch again. This time it went out and even though I managed to locate it with stiffening fingers, it wouldn't light again.

Bugger. And the others were back under the rubble, together with the energy bars and the water.

And yet, there was some light… Not a lot of light but it looked as though there might be a fissure in the rock ahead letting in sunlight? If so, was that a possible alternative way out? We humans will find hope in anything—or, at least, I will—and despite being soaked, frozen and terrified, I was able to pull Ben out onto the far shore of the lake. Then I sat down for an important time to cry; with fear and loneliness and shock. And for Jakob, almost certainly dead on the other side of the lake. And for Delyth and Ali who might have been caught in the landslide. And for me, who had had a dream that said I would die in the next forty-eight hours.

When I had cried my fill, the dust had settled and the rumbling stopped. I couldn't even see where I had come from but at least I *could* see. If this were some fucking Indiana Jones bastard movie, the light would probably be coming from underground worms that would guide me outside but the odds were against my being that cinematically-lucky.

I still had the chocolate in my pocket. A bar of seventy-per-cent plain which was not quite the comfort food I wanted but probably exactly what was needed. I ate half of it in case Ben should wake and be hungry. Then I made sure he was as comfortable as he could be—although both he and I were now terrifyingly cold—and left him to see how much closer to that light I could get.

I had to stop and put the sodden boots back on because the ground was sharp with stones, so that took some time and I simply couldn't get my fingers to tie the laces, but at least I did get my feet inside and I could squelch along in relative safety, although I couldn't say comfort.

'Any advice?' I said to Hero or any possible passing angel.

Be careful.

'Oh, great. Thanks.'

Be Buddhist.

That stopped me in my tracks. And then I remembered that there was a Buddhist technique of breathing yourself warm; the Breath of Fire. If I remembered correctly, you had to inhale gently and exhale quickly through the nose and then hold your breath for a few moments on the third exhalation. But I had to keep moving. Could I do the two together?

Not really, was the answer, but I gave it a go. It kept my brain busy focusing which blocked out a modicum of the fear.

'I've got you. It's okay, it's okay, it's okay' I said as a mantra as my body tried to object to breathing through my still somewhat blocked-up nose. I could feel Hero wrapping her wings around me, too, which also helped.

'Ben?' I asked.

You are doing this to warm both. His guardian and I linked.

So I tried harder and it seemed to work, just a little.

The light grew as well. After God knows how long, I came to a dead end except that there was a rockfall (oh great) and at the top of it, a clear fissure into what truly looked like daylight.

My fingers and knees were bleeding and my trousers torn by the time I had scrambled up there and I barely had the energy to push myself through.

The light blinded me. But there was warmth. Oh, heaven!

I scrambled out onto a kind of plateau and with weary and disbelieving eyes looked out at the ruins of the First Temple.

But it wasn't sunlight that was shining. It was an angel. The most extraordinarily glorious, bright and devastatingly beautiful angel you could possibly imagine. Exactly the kind of angel—or more accurately, archangel—you might expect to be the guardian of a great, yet fallen temple. The Supreme One; the light bearer itself.

'What the...?' I said to Hero.

Destiny, she replied and I knew that she couldn't prevent my destiny nor even warn me of it.

Shit.

Chapter Eighteen

OH HOW HAST thou fallen from the Heavens, O Lucifer, Son of the Dawn. That's the only mention of the greatest of all the fallen angels in the Bible. It's in Isaiah and it's usually translated as 'son of the morning' or 'of the morning star', referring to Venus. But it's *shakhar*. Dawn comes before sunrise and it's always darkest just before dawn.

All this ran through my brain while my heart and soul were held in wonder. It wasn't a wonder that I wanted to feel, given that I knew exactly what this was but, oh God, it was just *so* beautiful, so very gloriously elegantly exquisite.

And it had the wrong number of fingers on its hands. Like AI. Which meant it wasn't real: a depiction of Lucifer, not the whole being. That figured because it would probably be the aspect concerned with the corruption of this specific faith.

It was still bloody big, horribly powerful and almost certainly mean.

It would also be simplistic and banal which often made things even more dangerous.

Welcome, it said, looking at me with slanted aquamarine shark-dead eyes. **Let me warm you, human, for you are cold**.

'Only if you will do it unconditionally,' I said, my teeth chattering. 'Greetings to you, Spirit. I do not agree to any exchange between us without acknowledging that I fully understand the terms.'

Granted. You may be warm on condition that you hear my requirements.

'That is not unconditional. Hero?'

Safe to agree.

That's some new meaning of the word 'safe' of which I was previously unaware.

'I will hear your requirements. I do not agree to fulfil any of your requirements.'

You will agree when you hear.

'That is yet to be seen.'

But I felt warmth flowing through my body with mingled relief and concern that this being could get inside me already. And what about Ben?

He may be warm too if you will agree to one more requirement.

'Which is?'

You will open the veil to the Holy of Holies.

Yes. You must do this (Hero).

'I must?'

Yes. Destiny.

'But I'm not the High Priest.'

Oh I'm afraid you are, said the angel. **Consider yourself appointed**.

'By you?'

By me. I ruled this temple. I have authority.

'But I'm a woman.'

That was met by total incomprehension which, perhaps strangely, filled me with a moment of joy. A woman High Priest was acceptable to the angel of the Hebrew Temple, even if it were a fallen angel. That was fascinating.

Agree to the terms.

'I agree to open the veil to the Holy of Holies IF I am capable of doing so.'

You are. This agreement is made.

Hold, said Hero, as panic hit me. I had made an agreement with an aspect of Satan.

The Tester.

Yes, I must try and keep alert. And calm. At least I wasn't shivering anymore and hopefully Ben would now survive.

The angel did the equivalent of going 'ahem!'

'I'm listening.'

I require you also to enter the Holy of Holies, take me into the Holy of Holies and tell me what you perceive there.

Silence.

'That's it?'

Those are the requirements.

That was the moment that I finally understood temptation. I was being asked—maybe commanded—to do exactly what I wanted to do anyway, albeit without an accompanying fallen angel.

But surely I should never agree voluntarily to introduce—or re-introduce—a demonic presence to a deeply sacred place?

Necessary evil, said Hero.

'Really?'

Yes.

I paused and looked up, even though that just involved staring at the roof of a cave. This required a deeper prayer than consultation with a loving guardian angel.

'What must I do? Help me, God, please.'

It must have been a vision but it felt *so* real. The great Goddess was there, looking at me with love and concern and, yes, a smidgeon of sadness. She nodded. This *was* my destiny, then.

'Okay…' I said slowly.

Is that assent? Obviously the modern word was not familiar. Had this being been trapped here for thousands of years?

Yes. I felt a great wave of loneliness from it, mingled with a suppressed hope that was beginning to bubble. Possibly causing instability. Useful to know.

'It is assent. I will—if I can—open the veil and take you with me into the Holy of Holies. I will tell you honestly what I perceive. That is all.'

It is sufficient.

'May I ask you two questions? Without any further conditions.'

It didn't quite understand. Obviously everything in its mind was dual—tit for tat.

You wish to question ME?

'May the High Priest not do so?'

She may. It was reluctant to acknowledge that.

'Right. Why can't you go into the Holy of Holies on your own?'

It was as if I had thrown a flaming dagger at the angel's heart (assuming it had one). It gave a silent howl of pain and its colour changed from glorious to dirty pewter soused in congealed blood. For whole seconds it writhed and howled and retched and the echo of that silence was blood-curdling.

For a moment we were in darkness. Then Rus-El was standing facing me, in full Russell Crowe gladiatorial mode. He raised a hand and made a burning mark on my forehead—the Hebrew letter, Aleph, the mark of the High Priest. Then he turned and, as he did so, he took the full force of the blast of cold fury that the wreck of the angel spat at me. It was ill-disciplined enough to allow its rage to try and destroy the one being which could give it its desires. That, too, could be useful knowledge.

For a moment, I thought Rus-El had made it. He glowed scarlet and parried the hate with a stream of fire which did, indeed, stop the angel in his tracks. It calmed down and its colours began to reassert themselves back from vile to unremarkable and back into beauty. Light returned.

'Oh well done,' I breathed, before the scarlet angel went 'phfut' and quietly dissolved into a small pile of goo on the ground.

Oh well…

'Answer me,' I said, with a surprising amount of authority. The Aleph was still burning on my forehead.

Silence.

'I'm waiting.'

We broke away because you were given more authority than us, it said, quietly, in a voice of loathing. **We are exiled from the Holy One**.

'Oh.' Never before had I imagined what that must have been like. 'I'm sorry.'

You are what?

'I am sorry that you have suffered so.'

The angel nearly went purple with its attempt to understand this concept.

'It's a human thing,' I said. 'Empathy. The ability to try and understand how another feels.'

Why would you wish to feel pain which is not yours?

It was genuinely perplexed.

'So that we do not hate.'

This time it went almost avocado, like a bathroom in the 1970s.

You DO hate!

'When we have not evolved, yes. But when we evolve, we try not to hate. We try to understand.'

The temple angel had gone a very funny shape.

'Are you wounded?' I asked.

Yes, it gasped.

'Why did you kill my defending angel?'

Blocked access.

'Erm… hello,' said a rather nasal voice behind me. 'Bella?'

I spun round and saw Ben's nose. Ben was with it, obviously, and what had been already noteworthy was swollen and bloody. But he was clambering over the rocks and then standing upright and compos mentis and I was so relieved to see him.

He obviously had a waterproof case for his phone as he was using its torch but now, even with the strange fluctuating light from the angel, he could turn it off.

Strangely, I got a sense of disappointment from the angel, as though it was thinking **Wrong one**.

'Can you see the angel?' I said, first.

'What angel?'

'Okay. Listen very carefully—'

'I shall say this only once,' he said, quoting the old British TV series *'Allo 'Allo.'*

That made me smile. I'd somehow forgotten smiling and it felt strange.

I knew there might not be much time to explain so the words tumbled out of my mouth.

'Okay. Bathsheba's moths. Men passed out. Women okay. Delyth and Ali took Mo for help. Landslide. Jakob probably dead. Escaped with you across water. Temple ruins. Temple angel—fallen angel—here and communicating. Needs me to get into Holy of Holies.'

'Right,' said Ben. 'Not *all* right, obviously. Probably all wrong.'

At that moment, I thought I loved him.

'Where's the light coming from?' he added. 'It's not sunlight. From the angel?'

'Yes.'

'Then I must be able to perceive it. Greetings, Angel. I'm Benjamin Fairfax.'

'You don't give it your name!' I hissed.

Greetings said the angel. **Where is the other?**

'Jakob? He's probably dead,' I said.

Unfortunate.

'Yes. But why to you?' said Ben. Obviously he could pick up the communications. He seemed totally calm about all this.

Hungry.

'I see. And you could feed off his emotions? But not mine nor Bel's?'

Less so. He would be suitable high priest. But you must suffice.

'Oh jolly good,' said Ben. 'I presume you are the power that dried me off. Can you make my nose hurt less?'

'It only works quid-pro-quo' I said quickly. 'There'll be a price.'

Tired, said the angel. It really wasn't looking good. **Take me in**.

'I don't know how,' I said. But the angel pointed a grey-yellow-silver rather yukky hand towards the far wall of the cave. The stone there looked slightly different but it was hard to see.

'We need to look around here first,' said Ben, firmly. 'The High Priest needs to know the temple before daring to ascend to the Holy of Holies. You rest. We won't be long.'

He turned the torch on and began to look around just as though there wasn't a cranky archdemon present. 'It's surprisingly small, isn't it? I suspect the lake is covering the outer courts. Yes, look, there is a channel of water still running down the centre here. It's miniscule—I expect the water table has changed—but that's your living water. So, we are in the equivalent of the Court of the Priests here, are we? So where did the Menorah—or the Menorot—stand? And is the Ark here? And the Shew Table? Or have they rotted away? The top of the Ark should be real gold so it will be here if it wasn't hidden. The wood, of course, would have long gone.'

I stood aghast. The angel appeared to be obeying Ben in that it said nothing. In a rush I realised how much it needed us. It wasn't strong enough, thanks to Rus-El, to fight us. It would have to coerce and Ben Fairfax was a pretty formidable pocket of resistance to coercion.

Wordlessly I looked around me. I couldn't understand why the temple would be underground but maybe that was part of the Divine Feminine, honouring the darkness, the night, the unknown? I suppose that would make some sense.

'It probably wasn't underground; it probably sank because of seismic activity. But if it were, it would be easier to defend the treasures,' said Ben, reading my mind. 'Easier to stop the hoi-polloi observing everything. Not much different from Damanhur in Italy, and there's plenty of precedent dating back: Malta, Cyprus, Crete. They're called *hypogea*—Oh my God, Bel, look!'

It was a glisten of gold in the wall. Just like in Bathsheba's tomb, there were gold Menorot carved into the rock. It was hard to tell how many as there had obviously been temple-raiders here. We could see where gold had been chipped out of the wall but there was enough left to show what had been. It must have been magnificent.

'If there have been robbers, we won't find the Ark,' said Ben. 'I was resigned to that, I suppose. But this is still life-changing. Bel, we've found it!'

'Yes but will anyone find us?'

'Of course they will. The guys back at camp know where we went and Delyth and Ali will bring them. You can't tell me Bathsheba's tomb isn't going to be overrun by experts the moment they hear about it. They'll find us.'

Keep your word, said the angel, and I felt a burning feeling on my forehead. I put my hand up and traced the Aleph there.

'Hero?' I said.

Here.

'What should I do?' The idea of taking a demonic presence into the Holy of Holies wasn't a comfortable one, assuming I could find the way in.

Must be done.

'Really?'

No answer from Hero but **Keep your word!** From the angel.

'What is your name?' I said, turning and addressing it directly.

No name.

'Then I shall give you one.'

Keep your word.

'Word-El. That's your name.'

Behind me, Ben snorted.

'Damn it woman, that hurt!' he said.

Word-El. I am named.

Now I was at the back wall. The spring which dribbled across the floor came from a crack here. And the wall was strangely coloured as though stalactites ran down it. In the weird light they looked pale, turquoise, purple and red, the colours of the temple veil. I could just see the remnants of two human-built pillars set into the rock. On the left, one of dark stone for the feminine and one of pale stone for the masculine on the right.

'Wait,' said Ben, as though I was simply going to open that door with a push.

'I would like to come in, too. And you know only the High Priest may do so.'

'And it's possible there were two? One male and one female?'

'It's possible. Let's make that real.'

'Very well.'

I raised my right hand and drew the *Aleph* on his forehead. And, to my tired and nervous eyes, it seemed to glow on his skin.

'Does your nose still hurt?'

'God, yes.'

'It's dislocated. Shall I straighten it?'

'Oh shit. Yes. If you can. Dammit.'

'This will hurt.'

'I am aware. *SHIT! OW!*'

I pushed the septum back in place.

'You'll have two black eyes soon, too.'

'Ow, OW. Thank you. I think.'

And that was the invocation that made Ben Fairfax High Priest. Oops.

We stood side by side before the wall with the angel casting a shadowless light around us. Part of me wondered how it did that but it wasn't my main concern right now.

I put a hand up against the wall and spoke: '*Shemah Israel, Adonai Eloheinu, Adonai echad.*' Then Ben and I said the words again together.

And the rock moved.

Light poured over us. Bright, blinding sunlight. The Holy of Holies was open to the sun. It was a sink hole filled with flora and light.

What do you perceive?

I walked forward onto mossy vegetation. All around there was gold and straight ahead of me a great tree that glittered. A living Menorah of gold.

A living Menorah of gold, repeated the angel.

Oh my God, it was beautiful. The tree was gnarled and old. A surprisingly large laburnum cascading with golden flowers standing in the heart of this ancient temple.

'A living Menorah.' My legs felt suddenly weak and I had to sit down on the damp moss which partially covered a stream flowing from the roots of the great tree.

'*On each side of the river was the tree of life, bearing twelve manners of fruit, yielding its fruit every month; and the leaves of the tree were for the healing of the nations,*' said Ben softly behind me.

'But it's laburnum. It's poisonous,' I said, confused.

Ben started to say something and then stopped.

Poisonous? Said the angel?

'Yes.' I didn't understand. Glorious but poisoned? Any beast that ate laburnum seeds—was it ten seeds?—would die.

Tree of death? Said the angel. It was sounding remarkably more cheerful.

'Look,' said Ben, distracting me. 'It's not the original tree—doubt it could be, really. They don't live anything like as long as yews or olives. But see, here, behind it, on the wall, there's another Menorah shape. Looks like a Menorah was carved into the rock and a previous tree was escaliered there. How fascinating! That really supports the theory about goddess worship, doesn't it? All the poles and groves and trees that were cut down at the ending of this temple.'

I could see. And now my eyes were accustomed to the light I

could see the whole Holy of Holies was a glade of laburnums, an ancient forest of tree after tree growing and dying and giving birth again. Living gold. And yet, poison.

'The golden blood of the gods,' I said slowly. 'It was poison to humans.'

'That's Greek. We have no evidence the Hebrews thought the Lord had golden blood,' said Ben.

'No, but there are usually bleed-throughs in cultures and religions,' I said. 'That's the only thing that would make sense to me.'

I turned to the angel. It was looking a lot brighter now.

'I have fulfilled the bargain,' I said. Obviously one doesn't trust anything demonic as far as one could throw it but it needed saying.

You must eat of the tree, it said.

Angels don't like being laughed at—let's face it, who does? But the ridiculous irony of it was so much that my tired soul began to laugh that kind of hysterical heaving laugh that is hard to stop.

'You must be out of your tiny mind,' I said, as soon as I could speak again.

No, you will eat, it said. **You will die here slowly or eat now. To eat now would be a mercy**.

'You offer mercy?' said Ben, surprised.

The circle will be complete. Eat.

I felt an incredible pressure in my head as it spoke. Now it had regained strength the angel was capable of imposing pain just as it had been able to offer heat.

Eat, it said again.

The tree was awash with golden flowers but there were a few seed pods, too. Quite enough to kill the two of us.

'Bel,' said Ben, turning to me and taking my face in strong, rough hands. 'Do you trust me?'

'I don't know,' I said.

He sighed. 'Please. Trust me. You can trust me, I promise. Will you trust me?'

'I don't have a lot of choice, do I?'

'Well you could kick me in the groin and try running for it.'

Despite myself I smiled.

'Good girl. Trust me. Please.'

He turned to the angel.

'Will you eat?' he said. 'We will accept and eat but you must eat too.'

We do not eat. But it was yearning. And suddenly, I got it. Paul had destroyed a demon by choosing to die with it. And we could do the same. Oh dear God… do I have to?

'I expect it's like vampires, said Ben. 'You have to invite them in somehow.'

'Yes, with hate and fear.'

'Well, I'm not scared. And I'm feeling particularly happy, apart from the nose. I'm gloriously and wholly in love. What about you?'

A flicker of thought wondered if he were wholly in love with me or the temple but I didn't have time to examine it. The angel was hungry now; I could feel its energy circling us. Did it not realise that if we died, it would be taken through and away from this world too?

Don't think, whispered Hero.

I want to die, said the angel. That brought me up short.

So many years. So very long. Let me die with you.

To my surprise, I felt compassion. But I also felt strength.

'Then confess,' I said. 'Confess your corruption of this temple. Show us what you did to end the beauty of this worship. That is my condition. If you confess, I will help you die.'

The angel gave a cry, a sort of long howl and then the world dissolved.

Chapter Nineteen

His name was Joel and he was the eldest son of King Manasseh. He could only have been about sixteen years old and I watched him being carried into the temple, bound but not gagged. I think he was drugged; I hope he was.

I stood in a group of officials, some of whom were murmuring uncomfortably. Others had that kind of vicious excitement of people looking forward to something grisly or vile. Most were in brightly-coloured robes and I could tell that they were mages or wizards, rather than priests. I can't tell you exactly how I knew but it was obvious.

Yes, the heart of this temple was within caves, within a cliff. Not the outer courts, though. Those were familiar from my previous vision. The pyre had been built in the open air and around us were several altars. I knew Manesseh had brought other gods into the temple and, by the look of the statues, these were not pleasant gods.

The boy whimpered. He was semi-conscious. They laid him on the pyre which was oblong and packed with reeds and wood. The angel was there, too. It looked much bigger and even more beautiful than it had when I first saw it. I guessed it ate the energy of worship and of sacrifice.

'Enough,' I said. 'I understand.' But I was still there. And I was still there as they lit the pyre and as the smell of the smoke and the burning flesh filled the air. I found myself retching. It didn't matter that this had already happened more than two thousand years before; it was also happening now. And it was beyond horrific.

The excitement around me was palpable. The boy began to keen. Then he screamed once in a way that made me feel grateful I would never have to hear that sound in my dreams and then he was gone. It was just burning meat on a bonfire.

I saw the king's face, lascivious and greedy. There was no faith here; perhaps a fervent belief might have gone some way towards excusing the murder. But this was political; an excellent way to get rid of a difficult son and simultaneously appease some rather unpleasant gods and some even more unpleasant priests.

There were women there; I have to say that. I'd like to say they were disgusted by the scene but they were just as excited as the men. Yes, this temple was thoroughly corrupt and deserved to fall.

The angel was huge, vibrant and powerful. It ate the excitement and roared with joy at the sacrifice. It was both beautiful and terrible and if it shone into the minds of the people here, I suppose you could understand a fervour of worship. But it had nothing whatsoever to do with God.

The world tipped again and I was falling back into the world of golden flowers with Ben still beside me. In a flash of insight I realised I had sealed my own fate. The outrage I had felt at the gluttony of those people for human sacrifice filled me with anger and the demon-angel now had access to my psyche. It felt like being hit by a wet sandbag.

'Twenty each should do it,' said Ben, tipping out a handful of seeds from a blackened pod.

Only you, said Hero.

I tried to pull myself together, aware that she meant the only one bitten was me; the only one who needed to eat was me. Ben was probably right in that love was keeping him clear. Maybe he could escape?

'You don't need to eat,' I said. 'Save yourself. It only wants me.'

'No, we do this together,' said Ben. 'You do not get abandoned again.'

Word-El hissed and seethed at this pointless human-romantic interlude.

'We won't be found in time, will we?' I said.

'I doubt it,' said Ben, folding my hand around the seeds. 'If only a High Priest can get in here, no-one else will have access. I'm all right with that part. Nobody has to know this place exists. They'll have enough temple to fight over as it is.'

Neither of us said it or even thought it but both of us knew this demon had to be destroyed or it would poison anyone who came here.

We stood together for a moment and then Ben whispered, 'Phaedra Amabel Velvet, I love you.'

I guess that should have been a marvellously romantic moment but the idiot had now told the angel both our names. I wanted to break his nose again.

EAT said the angel. I expected to feel fear but instead I felt dizzy and strange. I could feel it questing within me to find something deeper it could hold onto even more tightly; some greater hatred or fear. And I knew from experience that it would almost certainly find something that my memory had lost. Something tried to rise up, something deeply shaming... but I could—just—close my mind to it because Ben still had his hand wrapped around mine. I looked into his eyes and saw only love.

It is now that matters; not then.

The angel-demon was losing energy. It was as much in my power as I was in its so when I ate, it would definitely eat, too. I could feel the echoes of the strength it had once had and I knew that it wasn't sorry for any of the things it had inspired. It was simply tired and old and abandoned and that was like carrying a dragging weight of pain and angry obsession. Human Bella might not want to eat the seeds and die but possessed Bella would have no option and would die in rage and resentment. Partially-possessed Bella might manage to die with love and surely that was the key?

But Ben?

'You don't have to do this. You can leave,' I said again.

'Rubbish.' And he threw the seeds into his mouth, chewed, made a face and swallowed.

'At least Adam did it first this time,' he said. 'Bel, please trust me. I know you have little cause to do so but please. Eat.'

So I trusted him and I ate. It looked like one of the prospective death dates would be only one day out...

As I swallowed, the demon swallowed too. And then it left me and soared overhead. It was gloating. My mind cleared; that odd horrific memory vanished.

Tricked you! Now I carry this poisoned chalice to the World! It cried. **Now I have the golden blood that will poison all of humanity. This is the power! This is the power of the Holy of Holies. Now you will die and I will rule!**

Then Rus-El rose up out of his spot of goo like the avenging angel he was and slapped it. It screamed and started spinning, spiralling, until it hit the rock wall to the left of us and fell in a nasty sticky pile of gunk on the grass. And after a strange moment of silence the resulting heap simply went 'phut' and one of the laburnum saplings fell over, missing us by inches.

Rus-El grinned and gave me the thumbs-up sign. Then he too disappeared.

What the...? My brain felt like suet. Hadn't there been some terrible memory redolent with shame? Where was it? I couldn't find it... And I wasn't dead or even dying.

'Oops,' said Ben. 'Turns out it wasn't laburnum after all.'

'*What?*' I stared at him.

'*Cassia Fistula.* The Golden Rain tree. Vaguely related to laburnum but this tree heals. It doesn't poison.'

'*What?*' I said again. 'You *knew* that?'

'I couldn't tell you,' he said. 'I had to let you believe it was laburnum. I'm sorry but it was the only way. If the demon believed it was poison it would eat it with us. I couldn't let it know it was facing healing, not death.

'You utter bastard!' I hit him on the chest. Again I was tempted to punch him on the nose.

'Yes. Sorry.'

Then we both sat down and indulged in some slightly hysterical laughter.

'Why couldn't it read your mind?' I asked.

'I'm in too much pain but I'm also too happy!' he answered. 'It wanted to eat the pain but I was the source of joy, too. Can't explain more than that.'

So was that it? Had the story ended? No of course not. You know all those movies where the hero and heroine think they've cracked it and something even worse turns up?

Of course the demon came back. No, to be fair, it wasn't the same one; this was its master. A horrible, greasy apparition that descended into the sink hole, filling our noses with the stench of corruption. It reminded me of the demon in the cathedral and it had the same intent.

You come to hell, it said, and as it stood on the mossy ground on the twisted approximation of feet, it seemed to take in a great breath.

Benjamin Fairfax, Phaedra Amabel Velvet Ransom, you die.

It threw dirt at us and we both collapsed, engulfed in a rolling hellfire, gasping in shock. And then the fire stopped, flared and rebounded, exploding the demon into a thousand shards of screaming agony.

'Fuck me,' said Ben. 'It worked.'

It *had* worked.

It had worked because the final angel got our names wrong. Only just wrong but wrong enough. It got our names wrong because Ben's legal name now was Benjamin Ransom-Fairfax and I was Phaedra Amabel Velvet Fairfax-Ransom. Only yesterday, in Jerusalem, we had taken wedding vows online with a minister from Utah and both signed the contract with what were our new legal names.

'We can get a divorce just as easily,' Ben had said. 'Non-consummation is the easiest way. But after what you told me about what happened in your cathedral in Exbridge it seems like a good idea to go all belt and braces on you.'

He had asked me to bring my birth certificate with me when I flew to Israel, simply by saying it might be needed. And he had arranged the marriage before I even got there. 'It could always be cancelled if you didn't agree,' he said. 'It was a marriage in name only with Maisie as well. It just seemed like a sensible idea.'

Oh boy, had it been a crazily sensible idea!

'What now, then,' I said after enough time had passed for us both to realise our brief, smelly visitor truly had gone, to calm down and start to think clearly again. Nothing else turned up to threaten or cajole us. It looked like the battle finally was won.

Dusk was approaching. The sink hole was now deeply shaded and growing colder by the minute.

'We keep as warm as we can; try not to think how hungry we are going to get and both hope—that's me—and pray—that's you—that Delyth and Ali got through safely. We can't hope for anything before tomorrow, now.'

'I have some chocolate,' I said.

'That's *my* idea of a high priest!' said Ben.

But miraculously we could hope for rescue sooner rather than later. After all, underground caves are dark day and night and rescue teams work as fast as they can. It wasn't all that long before we heard definite sounds of an engine. Probably an inflatable boat crossing the dark water.

'Quick,' said Ben. 'We don't want them to find this space, do we?'

'No!' We moved as fast as we could out of the golden sanctuary. I don't think Ben even looked back but I did and for a moment I thought I saw another angel, a strong, red, protective spirit that hovered within the tree.

Completed, said Hero, as the veil closed behind us and we stood in almost pitch blackness. Ben lit his phone torch again and aimed the light down the fissure in the fallen rock.

It was met with the sound of shouts. We were being rescued.

The Holy of Holies of the First Temple would remain a sanctuary until the time that another true High Priest could open the veil. Who knew what would happen to the rest of this temple; whether we would be allowed to do the surface excavations of the outer courts or whether it would be taken over by the Israeli authorities? Whatever happened, we had done our part and we could let what needed to be, just be.

And we had found Bathsheba's tomb, too, which was a *huge* archaeological achievement on its own.

Jakob's body was unearthed the next day and, as was customary for orthodox Jews, his parents refused an autopsy, so we buried him within twenty-four hours; standing respectfully with his family below the Mount of Olives. They were devastated, of course, but at least temporarily a little buoyed up by the knowledge that their son had been part of the greatest archaeological discovery of the century.

Mo and Ben had no after-effects from the moth-inhaling though Mo was less resilient than Ben who seemed to be vibrating with life. Maybe it was the healing *Cassia*?

It certainly was healing; though in the most disconcerting way.

The night after the funeral, I went to bed in the Airbnb I shared with Ali, both of us exhausted and simultaneously buoyed up and deeply concerned by the level of bureaucracy that was descending on our heads, not to mention the start of a media frenzy of disbelief, delight, speculation and horror in turn.

'Do you think this will do anything really to help the situation between Palestine and Israel?' Ali asked us all as we said goodnight.

'Almost certainly not.' said Ben. 'But it was the best we could do and it will at least ensure there are fewer excuses for the hatred. Israel has her original temple; maybe Islam can have the Dome of the Rock and even the Western Wall.'

'I wouldn't hold your breath,' said Mo.

'I'm not,' said Ben. You can do everything possible to promote peace but… well, people…'

I slept well that night but woke with a head clogged with thoughts. It was like an extraordinary weight of inconsequential tissue paper had descended. It didn't hurt but it was so *busy*.

I tried to check in with Hero but there was no contact at all which was disquieting. I avoided breakfast with the others and went for a walk to see if I could clear my head. With my brain still scrambling to cope it took a ridiculously long time before I realised what had happened. I could remember. I remembered everything. I remembered leaving my toy black panther behind when Jon took me away on holiday when I was nine and how I wept and demanded to go back for it. I remembered school. I remembered my childhood comics. I remembered looking over at Jon, sitting next to me, and realising he was dead. I remembered the moment I was offered a book contract. I remembered every house I had ever lived in; I remembered university; I remembered ordination; I remembered falling in love with Paul and how he would lace his hands in mine when we were in bed together. I remembered the first time I ate a langoustine in the south of France. I remembered breaking a toe in an archaeological dig in Turkey. I remembered being bitten by sharks. I remembered that I don't like sherry or Marmite.

How on earth do humans manage to stay sane with so much memory distracting them all the time?

As I shook my head, trying in vain to dislodge some of this suffocating clutter, I saw Ben in the distance and I knew for sure what had tried to wind itself into my mind in the Temple.

Ben Fairfax. My first true love. The man I met and moved in with while doing my first PhD. The man who jilted me at the registry office because he obeyed his family and, in the final analysis, couldn't marry a *shiksa* but *could* marry the Jewish woman his parents had selected for him. The man who vanished out of my life completely, breaking my heart the first and hardest time. The man I hadn't seen nor heard from for more than twenty years. The man whom I still loved when I foolishly married Galel.

My entire memory had returned.

So, Bella Ransom, time and space traveller, communicator with angels and demons and ghost-hunter, did die on the allotted day. It remained to be seen who would be resurrected.

'May I have a word?' I said as we met on the path back to the camp.

'Of course. What's up?'

'I've remembered. Everything. It must have been eating from that tree.'

'Ah. Everything? That must be… strange. Well then, the first thing required is an abject apology. Followed by grovelling. And almost certainly an annulment.'

'I… I… dammit Ben! I don't know what to say. I'm glad I know but I don't want any of the utter shit that comes with the memory!'

'I hear you. And I'm glad. There is an American surgeon called Bernie Siegel who said that if we all lost our memories overnight, every night, the whole world would be at peace.'

'I think he's right.'

'So, do you hate me?'

'No. I don't think so. Part of me wants to but I don't really think I can be bothered.'

'Oh, good girl! You always were amazing.'

I laughed ironically. 'Obviously not.'

'Oh Bella…'

'Tell me the story, Ben. Tell me about those missing years. Were you happy? I don't hate you—much—but I do need to hear the story, please.'

So he told me. Ben Fairfax, my first love, had been raised an everyday orthodox Jew, by which I mean they went to synagogue, benevolently despised those who were Liberal or Reform Jews but didn't have separate kitchens for milk and for meat and occasionally used the car on the Sabbath. Ben didn't really think about any of it much and it was only when he fell in love with this half-Hindu, half-agnostic that he realised the hold of his culture. That was why he never introduced me to his parents and why we spent our summer holiday abroad together on a dig and why he very rarely went home.

He asked me to marry him after six months and, both happy and confident, we booked the registry office.

Three days before the wedding, Ben travelled down to London to tell his parents. I knew something of the situation by then but I wasn't worried. Even if they cut him off, we were young, we were in love. What did they matter? We had the whole world ahead of us and they were simply stick-in-the-muds locked into the past. Ah, the arrogance of youth.

The visit was meant to be a *fait accompli* but somehow they reined him back. There was a girl in Israel to whom he'd apparently been betrothed since birth. It was true; he had conveniently forgotten. Eugenia was coming over in a few weeks' time and both families had agreed on a summer wedding in Jerusalem.

He couldn't tell me. There was one awkward phone call where he was obviously confused and distressed but I assumed it was just random family resistance. If they didn't want to come to the wedding that was fair enough; their being offended at the short notice was fair enough; objecting to his marrying a non-Jew was (I supposed) fair enough. He would turn up on the day, obviously. Not.

Later, he tried to contact me, presumably to explain.

'I did, Bella. Truly I did. I was so confused and upset—and weak. I rang you, I think, six times but you didn't reply.'

'Do you blame me?'

'No. But if I could only have explained... I did write you a letter...'

'That would be the one my flatmate tore up and burned before I could read it. But you couldn't have explained. Not to the me I was. Not after leaving me standing in my white dress with a bouquet of lilies tied with ribbon at the Registrar's office surrounded by our friends. 'If I remember correctly, you were a bit of a wimp back then anyway.' Unworthy of you, Bella, but it wouldn't be human not to attempt just one swipe.

Ben smiled. 'Yes, I was,' he said.

'So, did you marry Eugenia?'

'I did. Genia. We were married for seven years. She died in childbirth. Our son was stillborn.'

'I'm sorry.' That was true. 'Did you grow to love her?'

'Once I'd forgiven her, and myself, I liked her a great deal. She was coerced, just as I was. We understood that and we did the best we could with a situation we were both too weak to oppose. Tradition and family are very powerful.'

'I wouldn't know. I didn't have any.' I didn't mean to sound bitter. Bitterness felt strange. Without a memory, you don't experience a lot of it and I didn't like it. I shut up and listened.

Ben and Genia had lived in Israel for all their married life. Genia had had two miscarriages and found it very hard to carry a child. Her last pregnancy had been spent mostly in and out of hospital with pre-eclampsia and HELLP syndrome, leading to liver damage. Aaron was stillborn, eclampsia itself hit and took his mother within a few days.

'By the time I had recovered a little, I did try and seek you out,' said Ben. 'I found out that you were ordained which was, I admit, a little confusing.'

'For me too,' I said with a smile.

'And it didn't bode well for any reunion,' said Ben. 'Then I met Maisie on a dig. She really was a raddled old bat, but an entertaining and interesting raddled old bat, and we arranged our strange marriage. So, because she lived in your village, I plucked up my courage just last year and came to visit to see if we could talk.

'You walked right past me without even recognising me.

'Maisie told me about your accident and memory loss and I'm afraid I rather stalked you around the time of the trial, which is why I knew so much about it. I wondered about talking to you but the gossip was soon rife about you and the man who had rescued you...'

'Will,' I said.

'Yes. And I thought that if you had completely forgotten and had the chance of a new and happy life, I should leave you alone.'

'But you seemed to have gone on loving me.'

'Yes. I did. I still do. I'll quite understand if you want to walk away but I hope you don't. After all, I *did* marry you this time.'

I looked at him with more than twenty years-worth of exasperation.

'Too soon?'

'*Much* too soon.'

'Sorry. It's just that I hope, I *really* hope...'

'Yes?'

'I hope you might be willing to see if it might be possible to try again. That you might give me another chance.'

I walked away from him with a 'talk to the hand' gesture.

And the leaves of the tree were for the healing of the nations, whispered Hero in my heart. I could barely sense her but she was still a part of me. It was a quotation from the Book of Revelation, all about the ultimate happy ending and, at that moment, extremely annoying. I saw again the beautiful living golden tree in the Holy of Holies.

Ten minutes later I walked back.

'I might.' I said. 'But not now. Not yet. But I might. Maybe. Some velvet morning, when I'm straight.'

Obituary.

Amabel (Bella) Ransom, author, archaeologist and priest.
This controversial minister's role in the re-discovery of the first
Jewish temple both fascinated and scandalised the world.

Rev. Dr. Amabel Ransom, who has died at the age of 77, was both a contentious figure in the theological world and a renowned archaeologist. Ransom was born to an Indian Hindu mother and Scottish Presbyterian father. Her first book, *Mother of God*, chronicled the reverence for Nature and the Divine Feminine she claimed lay within the belief system of the early Hebrew peoples.

Ransom was ordained at the age of twenty-nine and was the Rector of the Tayford Parishes in West Devon for seven years where, in 2026, she became involved in the exposure of a paedophile ring including both church officials and senior police officers.

In 2027 she joined Professor Benjamin Fairfax's archaeological dig in its successful search for the grave of Queen Bathsheba, the mother of King Solomon, who built the First Temple of the Jewish people. In a remarkable series of coincidences, the team also discovered the remnants of the temple itself, leading to huge controversy within the Jewish nation as to whether these findings could be recognised as the true spiritual home of the Israeli peoples. While contention still continues after another thirty years it is remarkable to note the marked reduction of hostilities in the Holy Land since the discovery. The site is still a place of pilgrimage and worship, it having been established that animal sacrifice was not a part of First Temple practices. Ransom's part in that research and debate into sacrificial practices was seminal although her research into the possibility of First Temple priestesses is still not formally accepted.

Ransom's later autobiographical work, *Speaking With Angels,* where she wrote of a near death experience in her forties that led to her claiming to be able to converse with angels and demons and to visit the afterlife, was hotly debated and disputed in theological circles. She also wrote a series of children's books about angels which Netflix adapted into a much-loved television cartoon for children, *Rus-El and The Ghost Hound.*

Ransom spent the last thirty years of her life working in archaeology together with her partner. In her last interview, in 2043, she told how hard it had been to re-adapt to everyday life after her head injury had led her to believe she could converse with angels and ghosts for nearly two years. She strongly resisted links with angel 'experts' in the holistic world, claiming that angels 'don't chat and neither do I.'

Ransom's funeral will take place at St. Raphael's Church, Tayford and will be co-conducted by Rt. Rev. Lucie Cox, Bishop of London and a former curate of the Tayford Parishes, Rev. Robert Simmonds.

Typically, for such a controversial character, Ransom's eulogy will be given by her friend, 'the witch of Tayford,' Mrs. Alessina Bennett.

Epilogue

Alessina sat spinning in the corner of her sanctuary. It was late; the last embers smouldered in an ash-strewn hearth and flickering beeswax candles cast deep shadows around the terracotta-coloured walls. Outside, clouds scudded across a waning quarter moon and draughts slid through the uncurtained windows from hazy, speckled skies.

She focused on her thread, her body moving back and forth with the dancing of her age-spotted hands and the rhythmic pulsing of her foot on the treadle. Occasionally, she pushed her long, grey, plaited hair back over her shoulder before it found its way forward again, attempting to get caught up in the dance. She usually tied it up in a bun while spinning and she was wearing the wrong shoes, too, which made the whole process clunkier than usual—but she had her reasons.

In the corner of the room her totem animal, a ghostly-white barn owl, waited. Occasionally they spoke in swirls of soft colours.

All at once, Theodosia lifted her wings and flew up, through the cottage's ceiling and again through the thatched roof, taking Alessina's vision with her. Together they floated soundlessly down through the village of Tayford to its beautiful little Norman church where Bella's service had been conducted and attended by the Archbishop of York, Most Reverend Xavier Morel and the Bishop of Winchester, Rt. Rev. Alexander Dubois.

Bella was laid to rest in the churchyard of St. Raphael's and one final inexplicable event in the life of Amabel Ransom occurred when five hounds from the local drag hunt were found lying around her grave.

Theodosia landed on the roof of the Old Rectory. Snores from the now-retired Robbie could be heard through the open window of the home where he resided in a perpetual state of amazement that anyone would give him anything so incredible as a forever home. It was his in its entirety and every night he prayed fervently for the repose of Bella Ransom's soul.

That thought made Alessina smile; as if Bel would repose! She had spoken at her friend's funeral within the packed-out church about how Bel would be busy re-arranging heaven and insisting on better grades of ambrosia in the afterlife. Some of the congregation chuckled in recognition; some thought it was a frivolous eulogy and achieved a comfortable level of outrage that a self-acknowledged witch would even be invited to the old Rector's interment.

The grave was already covered with shoots of the first wildflowers of the year, lovingly (and illegally) transplanted from the verges around Alessina's cottage. In a month or so it would froth with celandines, three-cornered leek, pink purslane, herb Robert, wild violets and stitchwort. There was no stone yet, of course, but when it was laid it would simply have Bella's name—and later perhaps Ben's name—the dates of their births and deaths and the word 'Radiant.' There would be a separate plaque put up in the church.

The church itself had long been colder without its visionary Rector. Neither Lucie nor Robbie, nor their successors, had seen the angel at the altar so fewer celestial beings attended nowadays and the very fabric of the church seemed to sag a little. Robbie did return and do his best in the parish and his black rescue Labrador, Indie, who was blind and smelly and incredibly loving, filled in most of the gaps. All had long been safer and more easy to understand for those who still attended church in Tayford. The hordes who had descended for the funeral had long dispersed, the letters of condolence had been recycled and someone, of course, was writing a somewhat inaccurate and worthy book about it all.

Theodosia took off and circled the church, heading for home, and an echo of an angel reached up to her in greeting. *All is well; everything passes; this too shall pass; all is well.*

A soft sound drew Alessina's spirit sight and attention back into her body. She was still spinning and the soft *thrum thrum* of the wheel melded softly with air around her.

Gently, she stopped the wheel with her hand and listened. Yes, there it was again.

She stood, carefully, so as not to disturb anything and, blowing out the candles, lit an electric torch so as not to risk waking her sleeping husband and granddaughter upstairs with a brighter light.

She was in the hallway when the gentlest of knocks sounded on the front door and it took only seconds to open it and to adjust her sight again.

'Will I need a coat?' she asked with a smile that lit up her beautifully-lined face like a ray of sunlight.

'Probably not,' said Bella, smiling back.

The two friends held each other tightly for more than a minute before walking hand in hand up the stone paving that led to the little house's wicket gate and to the dark blue Fiat Panda parked just outside.

'Are you happy?' asked Alessina as she opened the passenger door, sat and fastened her seat belt.

'Incredibly so,' said Bella.

'Let's go then. I brought chocolate.'

'Marvellous woman!'

And then they were rising up as the little car took off for the solar system, the stars and the galaxies and the Work that will continue until the end of time.

One day, just maybe, you will meet them for yourself.